Library

of

Influence

Library of Influence

Book 3
The Lady Jane Chronicles

by
Reba Jean Smith

Word of His Mouth Publishers
Mooresboro, NC

All Scripture quotations are taken from the **King James Version** of the Bible.

ISBN: 978-1-941039-57-1

Printed in the United States of America
©2024 Reba Jean Smith

Word of His Mouth Publishers
Mooresboro, NC

www.wordofhismouth.com

Dedicated to the Ladies Matilda, Diane, Dana, and Constance. Thank you for being such godly influences in my life.

Sphere of Influence:

Sir Theo (husband)
Jimothy and Jac (sons)
Lady Matilda and Sir Reynaldo (family)
Lady Diane and J.D. (family)
Amy Lynne, Allan, Gabby, Ami (family)
Joe Nathan and Amika (brother and his wife)
Rae Anne (sister)
Lady Constance, Nobleman Tuck, Skye, and Daisy Mae
Lady Dana and the Emissary of Stone's Corner
Scarlett
Jenitta (church counselor)

Chapter 1

"Oh, what a day that will be when my Jesus I shall see, as I look upon His face...." sang Reba Jean to herself. Things were settling down, prayers were being answered, and all seemed well in her little world. The puppy was learning to sleep on its own, and the big dog was becoming less of a hassle. In fact, Reba Jean had a thought that might even have been from God. What if the big dog was sent to her to protect her from trouble? When she looked at it like that, she began thanking God for the big dog. Her stress level was way down, and she felt as if the anger and resentment were now a thing of the recent past. Her marriage seemed to be on good terms, and she was working on how she reacted.

Lady Constance was a frequent confidante and had given Reba Jean a printout of verses on how to have victory. Every verse was exactly what she needed—more treasure to collect. Reba Jean mused over her treasure collection. She began to think about how the secrets had been exchanged for treasure in the Library, but it couldn't just stop there. No, the treasure had to influence how she lived and how she interacted with others.

Reba Jean had begun writing the companion devotional to her previous book that very morning. Writing a devotional was a huge undertaking for her; she prayed that God would use this to help so many people who needed to understand how precious the Word of God and its riches were for their lives. She wanted to be anxious about whether or not she was doing a good job, or even if her second book would be approved by the publisher. Her anxiety was about to go into overdrive when the victory verse for this morning resonated through her mind. Joshua 1:9: *"Have not I commanded thee? Be strong and of a good courage; be not afraid, neither be thou dismayed: for the LORD thy God is with thee whithersoever thou goest."* With an exhale, Reba Jean settled her nerves and told herself firmly to remember to be still and wait on the Lord.

She was assured that she was to keep writing, keep teaching, and keep praying. These three things together would keep her busy and hopefully out of trouble. Reba Jean hugged this surety to herself as if it were a real thing she could hold. Tomorrow, she would go back to the Library and tell Lady Jane that book three had already come into her head and heart, well, at least the beginning of it. She didn't know why this surprised her; the first two books had happened that exact same way. For some reason, she had expected the third book to take longer, possibly even a year, to start writing itself. She giggled when she realized what she had just thought. In the Library, this is exactly what would be happening; books were always writing themselves up there in that mysterious meandering of her mind.

It was nearly time for bed, and she was reminded that she needed to write down some prayer requests that had been shared with her before she forgot them. Prayer was one of her most valued treasures, and it was both in the Library and the living room. She also needed to work on her actual prayer closet. She had tried the living room and dining room, but they were too distracting. She had even tried her husband's prayer closet, but it felt more like his and not hers. She just couldn't figure out why her old prayer closet did not seem to suit her needs anymore. She wasn't going to worry about it; she was going to pray and ask God to show her where He wanted her prayer closet to be.

Reba Jean wandered off to get her prayer journal and record those prayer requests so that she would pray for them that night as she headed to bed. She felt a snippet of another song lingering in the back of her subconscious. She wasn't sure what it was, but it was comforting to sense it lingering in the ether. Every morning, she would awake and literally be singing a hymn or chorus in her mind as soon as she reached a conscious state. That song, whatever it was, would be in her subconscious for the rest of that day. The next day would usually be a different melody, and she was looking forward to each morning to see how her mind and heart awoke to praise the Lord all on their own. Praise was becoming a living treasure for her. It surely did influence how she awoke each morning. Maybe she should start noting what song she awoke to each morning in her prayer journal! Then, she might be able to see if God was preparing her for her day in this specific way. She got excited when she realized that this subconscious jewel that she had been given might also be a weapon.

Awaking in the predawn hours, Reba Jean noticed that there was no song running through her head. She was shocked and upset. Had her voicing the subconscious thought negated its presence? She made a song come to mind, a Christmas carol of all things, and she sang it through until she fell back into a fitful slumber. Upon waking up the second time, another song was running through her mind, a vulgar worldly song snippet from her teenage years. Reba Jean was hopping mad! What on earth was happening to her lovely internal melodies of praise? Then, she focused on the snippet of the song that would not leave her mind. Laughing, she realized it was about chameleons. Well, no wonder her subconscious had brought that forth; she had been writing about chameleons in her second book.

Reba Jean spent the day talking to Lady Constance and Lady Diane about what the Lord had been showing her in her studies, both for the Library apprentices and her own personal Bible Study. It was so good to talk with like-minded sisters who loved learning from Scripture. Lady Diane had come back into her life in the last few months, and now they talked nearly every week. The treasure she had in these two women was so precious to her. They had such an impact on her walk with the Lord; she loved their influence on her and hoped she was a godly influence on them. She was still pondering the concept of the difference between something just influencing her or actually defining her.

After working on the second entry for the devotional, she reflected back on her day. Lady Diane had commented on how relaxed she had sounded. It was a relief to know that the calm and peace she was currently experiencing was evident to others. Her mind ran around in various rabbit trails as was usual for her. She only half thought about what that might look like up in the Library. All of this introspection had her leg jiggling again. She hoped that the Lord would use these trips down memory lane and into the meandering maze of her mind to be a good influence on her readers.

Tomorrow, she hoped to visit with Mardie, another precious sister of the heart. That phrase gave her pause; sister of the heart was such a sweet term for someone that God places in your life to help you mature and grow and guide you through your life with their prayers, wisdom, experience, and comfort. She had precious sisters of the heart, but her sister, RaeAnne, was the real sister with whom she spoke throughout the day. Their bond went back to childhood when they had made a pact to always be there for each other, no matter what. It was a fierce bond of loyalty, and Reba Jean placed great value on that blood pact.

Thinking about RaeAnne caused Reba Jean to send a note up to the Library. Lady Jane needed to be ready for when RaeAnne came to visit the innermost part of the Library. RaeAnne's avatar was Silver Wolf, and that persona could have interesting reactions from Lady Jane if she were not aware. RaeAnne had visited the Library many times but did not always let Silver Wolf loose out of respect for Reba Jean's concern for Lady Jane. However, Reba Jean thought it was probably time for Silver Wolf to be allowed to explore the Library.

Lady Jane received the odd note from Reba Jean, and she thought it very strange that Reba Jean would allow wolves into the Library, but even stranger was the fact that Reba Jean did not come to tell her in person. What could this possibly mean? An odd prickle on the back of her neck made her wary of this deviation from the normal protocol. Only Lady Constance and now Lady Diane had been allowed to visit the Library in recent days. The calm and peace had been so healing, but a wolf running around the Library, surely that would cause mayhem!

Lady Jane shivered as that prickle of fear slid down her spine. What would this visit entail, and why must it include a wolf? Still shuddering, Lady Jane looked to her left and then to her right; not seeing anything scary, she still bolted straight to her boudoir and dove under the bed covers. Such an irrational fear, she was sure, but she just couldn't shake it off. She struggled under the mound of covers, and her foot connected with a creature, which nipped at her in warning for upsetting its napping location. With a shriek, Lady Jane tossed the covers to the floor and checked her foot for any wounds.

A large, orange cat scowled at her and huffed off a few feet away to watch her with its glowing yellow eyes. It then re-approached her and sat down with its back turned to her, aloofly. If this is how she reacted to a stupid cat, how would she react to a wolf?! Lady Jane grabbed the note again, re-read its cryptic message, and decided she would tell Reba Jean just exactly what she thought of this whole wolf thing. The orange cat meowed and prowled around her feet as she tried to control her fear of the unknown avatar coming to visit. The orange cat continued to weave itself around her, and she began to get suspicious of it. Was this one of Reba Jean's, or did this cat belong to Captain Insidious and his ilk? Casting about for a way to discern, she thought about flinging some of the Water from the Living Fountain on it. However, no cats of any ilk liked water flung upon them, so that wouldn't help. She did not recall any Scripture verses about cats; the Ancient One was silent about how to deal specifically with somewhat domesticated cats. It only mentioned lions, and she did not think this small nuisance fit that category.

With a determined air, she summoned Reba Jean to the Library to identify the cat and to discuss this whole wolf visit.

With a distracted air, Reba Jean answered the demanding summons to the Library. She wandered in almost like a lost child and looked around at everything as if she had never seen it before. "Reba Jean! What is wrong with you?!" remonstrated Lady Jane.

"Oh, I was just trying to see what it might feel like for someone to visit who had never been here before. So many people only get to the atrium and never see the rest of this beautiful, amazing, mysterious place. It's always changing, as you well know," replied Reba Jean, sounding more like a tour guide than a resident owner.

Reba Jean perched on the edge of the Fountain of Living Water and dreamily ran her fingertips through the healing liquid. Lady Jane watched her with a petulant expression on her face. They needed to discuss this, and Reba Jean was acting like a silly woman in a daydream. The orange cat wandered over, and Reba Jean tentatively held out her hand and then rubbed the back of its neck. The cat was a bit wild; it wanted attention but was extremely finicky about how it received it.

"Reba Jean, is that one of your cats?" whispered Lady Jane. Reba Jean looked down at the cat lying on its back and purring, looking deceptively sweet and cuddly. "Of course, this is Mellow, but why is it up here in the Library?" answered Reba Jean.

Lady Jane let her breath exhale in a whooshing sound of relief. Okay, so this cat was a bit feisty, but it wasn't from the Nether Realm. She would just have to be a bit cautious in how she interacted with it so as not to get nipped or clawed. With that thought, a misty tendril tapped her on the shoulder. She shrieked and then giggled. Looking at the attentive tendril, she allowed it to write in a book that was nearby. Her eyes widened as she read what it wrote, a thought straight from Reba Jean that had not been voiced aloud or even telepathically to her.

Oh, it was a comparison of how the orange cat was much like Silver Wolf, a bit wild and needed to be handled with care, but nothing to fear. She sat there and gathered her nerve with only a margin of success. Hearing the pages of the Ancient One flip open, her eyes lit up, and she ran to the marble pedestal holding the precious Treasure. It had opened to Reba Jean's victory verse for yesterday. Joshua 1:9 *"Have not I commanded thee? Be strong and of a good courage; be not afraid, neither be thou dismayed: for the LORD thy God is with thee whithersoever thou goest."*

Lady Jane hung her head; she had let fear reign in her mind instead of asking King Abba for strength. She leaned over and hugged Reba Jean, but she still felt a bit out of sorts over this whole idea of a new avatar coming to visit. Lady Constance and Lady Diane did not bring their avatars when they came to visit. Sir Theo only had bees in his bear den of a Library. Why should Rae Anne bring her avatar to THIS Library?

Reba Jean looked at Lady Jane fully for the first time since she had been summoned into her presence that night. Why, it looked like Lady Jane might need some reassurance that Silver Wolf would not eat her. Maybe, though, she needed to rethink this visit from another avatar. Lady Jane had been through so much chaos and hurt in the last couple of months, not to mention all the years of trauma and drama. If Silver Wolf was just too much for her to adjust to right now, maybe only RaeAnne should come for a brief cup of tea as they discussed the treasure collection.

Reba Jean did not say anything to Lady Jane as she sat there and thought back to all the anger that had manifested in the Library and living room. There was great treasure to be had and kept, but the quest had been hindered greatly by the bitter emotions that had swirled around them. The Scripture said, "Be angry and sin not," however, she was sure that she had not followed that commandment. As she thought about this, the pages of the Ancient One started turning again. Reba Jean walked over to see what it wanted her to know. Romans 6:12-13 *"Let not sin therefore reign in your mortal body, that ye should obey it in the lusts thereof. Neither yield ye your members as instruments of unrighteousness unto sin: but yield yourselves* unto God, as those that are alive from the dead, and your members as instruments of righteousness unto God." She gulped as the pages flipped yet again, and golden letters swirled out and surrounded the two women as they stood there looking chastened and miserable.

These words from Colossians 3:12-17 embraced them as they knelt together and gave their fears and anger to the King of kings. "*Put on therefore, as the elect of God, holy and beloved, bowels of mercies, kindness, humbleness of mind, meekness, long suffering; Forbearing one another, and forgiving one another, if any man have a quarrel against any: even as Christ forgave you, so also do ye. And above all these things* put on *charity, which is the bond of perfectness.* **And let the peace of God rule in your hearts, to the which also ye are called in one body; and be ye thankful.** *Let the word of Christ dwell in you richly in all wisdom; teaching and admonishing one another in psalms and hymns and spiritual songs, singing with grace in your hearts to the Lord. And whatsoever ye do in word or deed, do all in the name of the Lord Jesus, giving thanks to God and the Father by him.*"

Verse fifteen continued to glow in a lovely, golden hue as they let His peace rule in their heart instead of the defeating emotions that so often consumed them. Reba Jean sat down on the floor under the Ancient One and let the words swirl their comforting peace around her. She mused about the last few days and how peace-filled and calm it had been. She had closed the book on her childhood issues but kept the treasures that she had collected from those years. Then she thought back on the consuming anger and resentment that had plagued her as she tried to hunt for more treasure. She was thankful that God had intervened somehow, and she had confessed that anger and resentment to Him.

Lady Jane was trying not to be anxious about Silver Wolf coming to visit. She didn't mind RaeAnne; she had known her all her life. Would Reba Jean give her armor to wear while the wolf was around, just in case? Lady Jane slanted a look at the peaceful Reba Jean and tried to keep that mantle of peace around her just a bit longer. Reba Jean sensed that Lady Jane was still intimidated by the thought of another avatar in the Library, but she knew it was more the appearance of the avatar. She had a feeling that if it wasn't a large silver wolf, then there wouldn't be such a mixed bag of emotions.

Reba Jean clapped her hands as an idea formed, and as such things were not unexpected in this amazing Library, there appeared over their heads the lovely formation of a tea party. Lady Jane looked up at all the dainty teacups and teapots and lovely plates holding tiny petite fours dancing around overhead and raised an eyebrow in silent query. "Lady Jane!" Reba Jean proposed an idea, "What if we had a tea party, you, me, Lady Diane, and Rae Anne?!"

"And Silver Wolf?" her voice trembled as she asked her mistress.

"You know what, my dear, maybe we should just let Silver Wolf hover in the ether like it usually does when I visit with Rae Anne. Then you won't have to really notice that it's in the Library."

Neither Reba Jean nor Lady Jane were dog people, so having a beautiful, large silver wolf was really intimidating if you thought too much about it. A tea party sounded like a lot of fun with the women who had such a long history together. Would Rae Anne and Lady Diane come to the Library? The women giggled together companionably and pretended to have their own little tea party, just the two of them. It was such a fun little deviation from their usual conversations.

Chapter 2

Reba Jean hugged her little avatar goodnight and headed downstairs to bed. She was still a bit troubled about the whole avatar issue that seemed to be viewed as a major disruption instead of a grand adventure. Hopefully, Rae Anne wouldn't be upset if Silver Wolf had to remain nearly invisible when they came to visit. As she prayed before she tried to go to sleep, she wondered what song she would wake up to in the morning and what the next day would bring.

Reba Jean woke up to a song of thanksgiving running through her mind, and that set the tone for the morning. Her Bible reading and study time seemed to be a warning that God was strengthening her for something that would happen soon. She paid attention to it and tried not to be dismayed at the thought of something else happening. She was so thankful for the peace that she didn't want it to get buried under the avalanche of life. She had started going back to her old prayer closet, and it had been peaceful, still, and healing; however, she realized that she couldn't seem to stay in there as long as she knew she should or wanted to.

She had a discipline problem. It wasn't that God wasn't there; He very clearly was. So why did she only spend moments with Him in the prayer closet? She knew she needed to explore this further. She had a feeling it was the closed door itself that seemed to make her feel closed in. She prayed all the time outside on the porch, in the car, and in the rest of the house, so maybe it was a personal, internal issue that she needed to conquer.

Reba Jean drove up to see Mardie, and they had a grand time catching up and discussing the books that Reba Jean had been writing. Another woman they were with suggested that Reba Jean come to speak to her church group about the book. That was an interesting invitation to pray and think about. Reba Jean came home and relaxed a bit, made some pizza for supper, and thought over all the conversations and things from that day. It had been a very good day, but 'peopling' still wore her out.

The sound of her husband's phone ringing and the cryptic replies had her curious, and then her husband called her into his office. The ministry that they had just started helping in again, after a few years, wanted them to take on greater responsibility. Was this what the Lord had been warning her about leaning on His strength for? She was desperately going to need His strength; she did not like to be a leader, supervisor, or person responsible for large undertakings. She knew the prayer closet was going to be a necessity, and she needed to use it and get past the closed-in feeling it gave her.

Scrolling through her messages and social media, she noticed her publisher had posted a daily devotional about treasure. Of course, that piqued her interest, and she loved his insight. He encouraged her to weave it into her book and or devotional. She loved finding treasure in God's Word; that would be a lifelong quest for her. She looked at her notes for the devotional sitting next to her and knew she needed to write the next entry. She hoped book two and its devotional would be approved by the editor and publisher. She was trying to practice patience as she waited to hear what they thought. Either way, she would keep writing; it would burst out of her in some form or another if she didn't. The orange cat came back and meowed for attention; she ignored it as she typed another sentence, only for it to sink its claw into her leg, causing her to yelp in pain.

Growling in displeasure, Reba Jean stood up to go clean her fresh wound, thanks to that grumpy cat. She wasn't sure what the spiritual lesson was in this, and she really did not want to apply anything except antiseptic. What a way to ruin a good mood! She now had a stinging hole in her leg, a whining puppy, and a cranky cat to distract her just when she was going to delve into more treasure.

Time slipped away, and soon, Reba Jean found that she had not written in the devotional or in her book for weeks. Instead, she had binge-watched an old show or scrolled endlessly through social media. Oh, she wrote scenarios and devotionals in her head but did not take the time to type them out. She allowed many things to hinder her from what she knew she was to do. In fact, she engineered some of them on purpose.

It all came to a showdown between her and the Lord a few weeks into this habit. He consistently convicted her of her need to be doing the necessary things and not be engrossed in mind-numbing pastimes. She wrestled with her flesh and her desires for much longer than she knew was needful. Finally, she surrendered to the Lord those things that were hindering her from spending time writing or praying. Some of her excuses were valid, like the Velcro dog or the distracting husband. She just needed to pray her way around those hindrances. Sitting down a few days later, she took the time to write more devotional entries. She found out her second book had been approved by the publisher, and Lady Diane began making weekly phone calls to her. Those weekly phone calls were comparable to counseling sessions, and Reba Jean used them as such.

Skye was actively reading the first book in the series and providing feedback, which was a blessing and an answer to prayer. Lady Constance became even more of a source of fellowship and a spiritual resource for Bible study and convicting insights. Sir Theo was amassing a collection of study books from various authors on prayer, and now, together, they had a lot of studying to do. She did not want to feel daunted by the stack of books waiting for her to read and glean and grow from, but if she kept being distracted and hindered, those books would only seem to pile higher. Consistency needed to have

21

victory over complacency and dedication over distraction. All this she was well aware of and often convicted of, yet it was much harder for her to put into practice, even with determination.

The treasure collection in the Library was probably collecting dust, for all the time she spent studying each piece was next to nothing. She needed to go check on Lady Jane, but it was time to make supper for her husband, and she was feeling a bit antsy. She was still having withdrawals from the addiction to electronic entertainment, so instead of escaping into the usual routine, she went to the kitchen to start supper. Mentally chastening herself for wanting to become a TV zombie again, she tried to pinpoint where her restlessness came from. There just seemed to be too many possible causes to pinpoint any one in particular. She was not necessarily worn out, but the constant battle with the flesh and her own preferences did seem to be overwhelming her. She had already had a good cry that morning, and that had helped the emotions, but she had a feeling that her desire to escape into a TV show was just to numb her mind from thinking about everything that was causing her stress.

She had been listening to the hymns again today and was struck by how some of them were worded, "We should never be discouraged; take it to the Lord in prayer," for instance. Suddenly, after years of finding encouragement in that phrase, she took it the wrong way and wondered at the way it sounded like it was wrong to be depressed or discouraged. Oh, she was well aware that it was just her mindset today, and there was nothing wrong with the words to the hymn. Hmm, she began to think that was possibly the root cause of all her emotional upheaval; she was getting discouraged. Discouragement often led to depression, of which she did have infrequent, mild, short bouts. Taking it to the Lord in prayer helped, but she wanted clear-cut answers and immediate relief. This did not happen as often as she personally expected. Maybe it was even likely that her immersion into electronic entertainment had jaded her outlook. She had too much going on, and she just needed a break, which is why she often hid in electronic escapism.

RaeAnne would blame the Syndrome, but Reba Jean did not want to be obsessed with all the things that might be wrong with her or her ability to function through life. She wanted victory over everything and everyone. Sadly, she had a feeling the biggest victory she needed was over herself. Sure, her husband, the animals, the finances, and the ministry all played into her busyness; she still had to fight for sanity just with those issues. Too often, she felt like she was asking God to remove these things from her life instead of asking for His help to get her through it all.

Maybe a trip to the Library would help her let go of the stress and concentrate on the treasures... if they had not been stolen by pernicious pirates. She had not even relieved Lady Jane of the fear of Silver Wolf; she was probably hiding under the bed these past few weeks, shaking and trembling in fear. Reba Jean scowled at herself; what sort of friend or librarian had she been lately? She served supper to her husband, and since she had been on a different meal schedule, she was now free to run up to the Library.

Her stomach was already in her chest and threatening to strangle her as she climbed the stairs to the Library. Nausea increased, and she felt dismay wash over her as she opened the door with a trembling touch. It did not resist her entrance, and that brief relief was yet not enough to assuage her trepidation. Just inside the door was a small receptionist desk with a steaming cup of creamy coffee on it, awaiting her. The desk and its contents were a pleasant surprise to her, and she felt her stomach settle back down as she took a sip of the creamy brew. Off in the distance, she could hear a lecture playing in Sir Theo's office; the puppy whined as it sensed her presence. It had been with its master in his Library and had briefly left her alone. Off in the distance, the big dog could be faintly heard as it voiced its discontent at being alone outside. The Velcro puppy found her and began its persistent whining, and she huffed in frustration.

She draped a wrap around her shoulders, stepped into the portico, and inhaled, then exhaled. Her eyelid began twitching, and she knew she needed to calm down even more. Again, she inhaled deeply and then went to see what Lady Jane was up to. The thoughtfulness of the cup of coffee still stuck with her. Then, the sound of the lecture shut off abruptly when Sir Theo appeared in the archway between their two libraries. He rubbed her shoulders and gave her a brief caress. That helped a bit, too, along with the puppy following him back down to the kitchen in hopes of some handouts. She felt some of her stress ease out of her even as the puppy followed him back to his office, and the sounds of the lecture resumed.

The nausea tried to resume as she began meandering around the Library with no real thought as to what she was even seeing. She checked her coffee mug, thinking that it was empty, only to find it still had some more coffee in it. That gave her pause as she wondered if this was something that was new to the Library: bottomless coffee cups. She almost giggled; it was a Library, not a children's storybook world, or wait, wasn't it that as well? That giggle seemed to be the cure for the nausea, and she felt a smile reach her lips as she settled down on a chaise lounge and sipped her coffee. It wasn't long before she was finally able to look around. The lecture droning on was a bit annoying, and it seemed to echo loudly through her Library from his adjacent one, but she knew this was yet another distraction that was testing her. That reminded her that her lack of patience was probably part of the issue. She was supposed to be collecting this treasure from the Overseer, but she did not seem to have the patience to let patience grow. Her next sip of coffee found it cooled, and she nearly spit it out; now, there was a very applicable lesson. The sound of the lecture stopped, and Sir Theo and the puppy exited yet again, but the quiet and calmness that ensued were exactly what Reba Jean needed.

She set the coffee mug down and sat up straight as if about to go on a mission. Yet, she did not move; she just used her eyes and ears to discern what was going on in the Library.

She wanted to observe and familiarize herself with any and all changes before she did anything. Lady Jane still had not made her actual presence known, and Reba Jean refused to let that irritate her. The big dog woofed again, and Reba Jean wondered if she was going to once again be pulled back into the reality of the zoo before she could even tend to the Library.

Giving in to the inevitable, Reba Jean went down and back outside to tend to the dogs. The big one was hungry; it did not appreciate the rationing that they had tried to institute to help it lose weight. She fed it again and stood in the wind as it whipped around her. Coming back in, she and the puppy ascended up to the Library again. Sir Theo was talking to her from his office. It should have been companionable, but Reba Jean was still feeling a bit over-sensitized. Wandering around aimlessly, she began chewing her fingernails off. She always did this when she was stressed; no amount of coffee or caresses changed that. She did know that peace and quiet helped, but she was sorely on short rations for those. The Velcro puppy jumped at her leg and began to whine; she thought she was going to cry as the nausea rose yet again up into her throat. Noticing that she had chewed one nail so much that it was now bleeding, she stuck it in her mouth and scowled. Looking down, she noticed a scrawny, black cat coming towards her. It was one of Conté's cousins. Conté was short for discontentment, and she was very much aware of its influence in her life lately. The cat rubbed against her leg and then wandered off out of sight. She began to chew another nail as she heard a scurrying sound in the next room. Was it a rat? The puppy went to investigate, and even that was more of a relief. She soaked in the moment of quiet that ensued, with only the tapping of keys from the other Library could be heard. She rubbed her chin, checked her bloody finger, and then decided she needed to find Lady Jane before this trip to the Library was wasted.

Lady Jane had spent weeks by herself. She was fine with this; the living room needed her mistress more than she did. She was not unaware of all that was happening; she just chose not to be involved in the middle of it. She was glad that the dream room was no more than just a computer console that no longer involved her supervision. The cracks in the floor only seemed to let in steam and not rats, and the archway between the libraries was still sealed tight. The only critter that she really had to watch out for was the bristly Conté who liked to leave quill-like hairs in her as he brushed by.

The puppy could be heard fussing at someone, probably at Reba Jean, but Lady Jane stayed where she was. She was still concerned about Silver Wolf, and all the tea parties in the world would not dissolve that fear. Hearing some pages flipping, she cast her eyes out towards the Ancient One as It beckoned to her. Exiting her little hideaway, she met Reba Jean at the Ancient One as It flipped Its pages to Nehemiah 8:10 and wrapped golden strands around them drawing them together and to Itself. *"Then he said unto them, Go your way, eat the fat, and drink the sweet, and send portions unto them for whom nothing is prepared: for this day is holy unto our Lord: neither be ye sorry; for the joy of the Lord is your strength."* Together they studied the chapter and those words, and Reba Jean knelt on the floor and let the peace of God wash over her. Her visit to the Library was beneficial, after all.

The nausea was still there, along with a tired feeling, but she did not feel as overwhelmed as she had been all day. She hugged Lady Jane and told her not to worry about Silver Wolf; she did not think that the visit was going to happen any time soon. Lady Jane asked her why RaeAnne had chosen a wolf as her avatar, and Reba Jean speculated that maybe it was because she wanted something that made her feel secure and protected. She also speculated that maybe Silver Wolf was not even the avatar, but just something that RaeAnne liked as a companion, just like Reba Jean's blue butterfly. Lady Jane thought that over for a few minutes and felt her fear of the possible unknown dissipate.

The puppy sulked on the carpet near them, and the big dog woofed its lonely question yet again. Reba Jean had fed it some more food and had even let it run around in the den downstairs for a few minutes, but it was not content, no matter where it was or what it was doing. Reba Jean definitely could draw parallels to that. The Library settled down to moments of quiet followed by moments of amicable conversation between the two Libraries. The Ancient One had calmed most of the overload of stress and frustration as It usually did.

Their two heads rested upon each other as they sat in quiet companionship together, just she and her little avatar of the Library. The puppy whined at Sir Theo, and Reba Jean inwardly smirked that at least he was understanding what a Velcro-type puppy it really was. Reba Jean still felt nauseous and knew that she needed something to calm her innards, even as her heart had been calmed by the Ancient One. Sir Theo exited to get ready for work, and Reba Jean followed him to see him off. She smiled at Lady Jane and bid her farewell as Sir Theo accidentally stepped on the puppy, and the room erupted in yelps.

She calmed the puppy, saw her husband off to work, brought the big dog in as a storm was brewing, and then decided to curl up in a chair for a little while. She had a ministry responsibility in the morning. She had been volunteered or, as Lady Diane described it, "volun-told;" it was still a struggle with her as she did not want the responsibility if God had not called her to do it. However, all of her previous ministries had started the same way, so she had a feeling that it was more about her "want-to" and less about what God did not want her to do. She hoped that feeling would resolve itself soon.

As days went by, Reba Jean kept thinking of things to write, only to find she had already written them. She was still fighting with Conté, and she felt some of the old feelings of anger bubbling under the surface with resentment. All of her talk about accepting the zoo she was now the keeper of never lasted long enough for her to totally release the stress that it incurred. She was tired of being a zookeeper and tired of always feeling like she was at the beck and call of everyone around her. It sounded very selfish, and she knew most of it stemmed from her lack of adequate sleep. She did not want to take any sleeping aids and had even stopped her new medication, as that seemed to make things worse. Who was she mad at? Reba Jean had been reading all about forgiveness, and she had mused that it did not seem to apply to her right now. But if she was honest with herself, it might apply more than she realized.

She did not want the dogs, or maybe she just did not want their constant dependence on her. That was it; she wanted the dogs to be more independent and not need to be in her face and space constantly. That was why she preferred cats; they were much easier to take care of and were not always so never-ending needy. Clasping her hands, she sat for a minute to do some real analytical soul-searching. Her husband had taken the puppy outside with him and had encouraged her to have some time alone. She took that as time to write, for that was therapy for her. When she heard the puppy yelping as it had gotten away from its master, she grabbed her shredding nerves and ran up to the Library. She needed peace and quiet!

Entering the coolness of the dimly lit atrium, she shivered, feeling half fear and half relief. She was trying to hide from people, puppies, and life. Reba Jean did not search for Lady Jane or call to her. She just wanted to be alone with the Ancient One, the heavenly artifacts, and the collected treasures. Bowing her head into her hands, she rubbed one of the scabs on her face that had arisen yet again. She thought they were caused by radiation from her phone, but maybe they were also exacerbated by stress. Raising her eyes, she let them wander around the area while she sat in a crumpled heap. She giggled when she thought about her eyes wandering around, as if they were independent of her body. The blue butterfly flitted through the golden glittery dust emanating from the sunlight cascading through the beautiful iridescent windows above.

In the distance, the sounds of the lawn mower starting up almost jolted her, but she refused to be distracted from her escape. Inwardly, she felt as if she was holding herself together as tightly as possible. The sounds of the lawnmower came ever closer and drowned out any other sounds, except, of course, the yips of the puppy. The puppy was terrified of the mower, and even though it was safely in the house, it was not in the comforting arms of its mistress. Reba Jean could always draw spiritual applications from this, but she did not want to think about how she was too much like that recalcitrant puppy.

Sitting cross-legged on the floor, she leaned over into a curled-up ball again. Yes, it seemed that her problem was probably not enough sleep and not enough personal time. So, what could be done about that? She was a grown woman, and yet she just wanted to run away from the home that was no longer her oasis. She felt tears inwardly at that, but none came out. Her eyes landed upon that desk at the entrance, and she let her gaze roam over the book titles that were collected upon it. There was her Scripture printout for her victory verses over thoughts, temptation, fear, and discouragement. She needed to get those written into a devotional format. Another book was the *Prayers and Promises of God*, *31 Days with God*, her favorite, *Just a Minute Devotional*, her Blessing Book that had not been written in, yet again, a notebook full of notes and Bible study entries, and still another book about Jesus is Calling…the devotional, *the Range of Grace* was the last thing to catch her gaze. She had plenty of resources, she could write, she could be thankful, she could have the joy of the Lord as her strength, so she wasn't bereft of help; maybe she just needed a nap.

Still holding herself, she began to rock back and forth slowly on the floor. The mower and the puppy seemed to remove any semblance of escape or peace that she had hoped to gain by running to the Library. A breakdown was the last thing she needed, although maybe she should just have one and get it over with. Stress seemed to hang over her like a heavy blanket.

Stress was a huge influence on her, but it now seemed to want to define her life. Stress was similar to anxiety, fear, lack of trust, worry, but she didn't feel those; she just wanted— what did she want? She waved her hand, and the breeze wafted a few tendrils over to the desk, and the page of Victory Verses was gently placed on the floor near her. She read her notes about the verses that dealt with discouragement.

Almost like an invisible hug, she felt a little bit of hope wrap its arms around her, she read the notes again and tried to ignore the sounds of the puppy and the mower. She was in no mood to write any devotionals on these verses, much to her dismay. She relaxed her body and leaned against the cool marble of the base that held the Ancient One. She exhaled, kept her eyes closed, and prayed that the peace of God would rule in her heart. Instead, the puppy's cries reached a soprano chord and she felt her chest tighten. It had not even been an hour yet, and the Library was not going to be her oasis either. The tears came even nearer the surface, and she felt overwhelming fatigue wash over her.

Staring off into the dim recesses of the Library, she felt that her stress was creating a monster, and she did not know how to vanquish it! The world's ideas of relieving stress did not seem to help hers. Rubbing her arms, she felt goose flesh arise. She was sure there was a monster hiding just beyond her range of sight. She knew it was stress, even if it went by another name. It was kin to Conté, and she was in real trouble!

She wandered out of the Library down to the rest of the house, turned the TV on, and sank back in the recliner with the whining puppy. The crime show soon lulled her to sleep, and the nap, albeit short, seemed to settle her a bit. She made supper and fielded some phone calls from another concerned librarian who needed a sounding board. Her husband, after his hard work and yard care, was still antsy, and he ran off to the store. With quiet restored, Reba Jean sat down to write a bit more. This whole stress thing, along with making time or figuring out how to write, needed to be resolved. She told the puppy "no" yet again, and this time it flopped at her feet and pouted quietly.

Would it be possible to go back to the Library and slay the monster before it grew too big? She looked again at the copy of the verses on discouragement. Maybe she needed verses on contentment instead. The only one that resonated through her mind right then was … godliness with contentment is great gain…" Reba Jean wondered if her lack of godliness was the cause of her lack of contentment. It grew dark around her as she typed, save for the light of a lamp. She didn't want to make any abrupt movements and get the puppy all wound up again. She wondered what sort of monster was growing in the Library upstairs. Her fingers paused over the keys; the puppy whined, and she sighed. The puppy became insistent again; she saved her work and slumped in defeat.

Reba Jean needed real help, and only prayer was going to fix this, so she just had to keep praying and to keep trusting God to help her deal with this issue of the zoo and its stress on her. Sitting on the swing outside, she thought through all the ways she had researched to alleviate stress.

She walked about an hour every week with a friend; she was in her Bible daily, she was working on praying more and studying more, she listened to the lovely hymns; there were the weekly phone calls with Lady Diane, and the daily conversations with her sister. The sleep was getting better, her careful watch over her tendency to binge eat from stress or binge-watch TV was being dealt with, what more could she do? She was outside getting more fresh, pollinated air than she ever wanted thanks to the puppy. She found herself physically shrugging her shoulders. What do you do when you are doing everything you are supposed to do and it's just not enough?

Chapter 3

The monster in the Library was growing, and it often ricocheted off the walls whenever it careened out of control. Reba Jean was aware of the snarling creature; she had even discussed its appearance with Nobleman Tuck and Lady Constance. They were aware of such a creature that was like a cat that had morphed into a rat, or was it a rat that had clashed with a cat-like creature and became a mutant? Their vivid description depicted a horrific mental image that caused her to start finding ways to keep it under control. She had read somewhere that people thought that resentment wasn't from anger or frustration but from jealousy. She totally disagreed with that, and her lack of contentment seemed to be intertwined with this resentment.

Weeks passed, as Reba Jean went through the motions but felt like she was just existing, not enjoying life. She had a real sit-down session with God one night, as usually happened whenever she just had no real answers or solved problems. He brought up the memory of a recent sermon where it was stated that the flesh has influence on us but no longer had dominion (control) over us.

As she flipped through her other sermon notes, she saw such notes as "endure hardness as a good soldier of Jesus Christ", "bury your old man, forgive, forget, forge ahead", and that led her to 1 Peter 4. She had always thought that this chapter was about persecution, but wasn't the constant daily battle against the flesh a fiery trial? Her problem was that she expected complete and total victory over each of her battles and never expected them to bother her a second time. As a good soldier of Jesus Christ, she needed to look at each day as a day of victory, whether it was over a recurring issue or a new attack of the flesh or the devil. This was all well and good, but she had to practice it daily.

Sir Theo was pretty pensive for a while, and Reba Jean knew he was struggling with his own battles. One morning, as they drove to the ministry outreach that they both helped with, he shared that he thought that his roadblocks in prayer and Bible study lately might be because they were not having shared time in God's Word and prayer together as a couple. They had rarely had a shared time in all of their years of married life. It had been Reba Jean's prayer burden for years, especially lately, with her husband getting into studying the Word of God and praying like he never had before. She was thrilled and inwardly thanked the Lord for that answer to a long-time prayer.

This new victory would have a definite influence on her life from this moment onward. She was also aware that this could become a battlefield, which is what it had been while they had been courting. Hopefully, maturity would replace that feeling of competition or condescension and frustration that had been prevalent decades earlier.

General Nefarious had amassed his troops months ago, ready for a massive assault on the Library. He had turned around to share his strategy with Captain Insidious, only to find that the sneering underling had left his side to handle things in his own way. General Nefarious, albeit eager to have a final cataclysmic showdown, had not reached his level in the Nether Realm by being ignorant or unobservant. Captain Insidious was slowly and steadily rising in the ranks because he tried different types of attacks and played the long game. He never seemed to want his victims to be defeated just once, but daily. The general studied his notes and knew that he needed to take a similar strategy when it came to the Library.

Calling a council of his best scouts, he gathered them to discuss their intel and ideas. It was noisy and chaotic, as anyone would imagine when minions of chaos and anarchy gather together. The scouts reported that there seemed to be one of their morphed mutants still in the Library, but its success was yet undetermined. They also mentioned that Captain Insidious was plotting how to steal treasure that was being stored in the Library. He had been walking around like he was some sort of pirate lately, talking about the big heist he was planning.

Insecurity felt as though he had more success by attacking those around the Library; their lack of confidence and condescension seemed to have a greater effect on the hostages in the Library. Yes, he considered Reba Jean and Lady Jane to be hostages under their own roof. Doubtful and Anxiety had run numerous attacks on the Library in various forms; however, it seemed as if they were constantly overcome by some unseen celestial force. This force seemed to act as an invisible shield, and they just had to keep up the barrage. General Nefarious was well aware of that unseen shield; it was called FAITH. Biting his lip in consternation, he tasted the bitter gall that seeped forth as the thought of that shield that the Library seemed to have erected around it.

General Nefarious heard from Fear next, who stated that his attacks were not as successful as before; he kept getting cast out of the Library. General Nefarious grimaced again; he was well aware of what was being used to cast out Fear. The enemy from the Celestial Realm had a weapon formed from perfect love. A snarling scout shot up his clawed finger seeking attention, with permission to speak granted, he mentioned how Captain Insidious had been plotting on how to steal hope from the Library. He had heard that the Celestial Realm had warned that "hope deferred maketh one sick".

General Nefarious thought about this bit of scuttlebutt from inside the Library. Should he join Captain Insidious in his plot to burglarize the Library, or should he work on making that mutant inside the Library grow into something inescapable? Maybe he would just work both angles. He would align himself with Captain Insidious and pilfer the treasures, and also continue working to destroy the Library from the inside out.

A scout came slithering into the council session as it was wrapping up its reports from the various other minions. The glint in his slanted eyes caught the red glow from the fire that was used to arm their weapons. General Nefarious gave him permission to give a late report from the Library. "That strip of a female is doing some sort of victory celebration. It seems she and her big galoot of a husband are going to 'pray together'!" he snorted and laughed derisively, and the whole council joined them raucously. The General stroked his bewhiskered chin and was quiet as the minions caroused around him. Yes, Captain Insidious was probably smarter than he was given credit for, the long game would be best, mused the General inwardly. Time would tell if this new prayer thing would be a non-starter or a real detriment to his daily assault on the Library and its hostages.

Reba Jean was half giddy and half scared of the first prayer time together with Sir Theo. Would it actually happen? What WOULD happen? Was this the answer to her prayer issues, to his? She felt a knot form in her stomach and her head began to ache. She hoped it would be a huge boost to their spiritual walk and to their marriage. Oh, how she hoped it would help her resolve the stressors that plagued her daily. Reba Jean also knew that the mutant growing in the Library needed to be vanquished before it grew out of control. She also had to keep treasure hunting, although she was still finding a nugget here and there.

Sure enough, that first night, nothing happened, well, not nothing, a good heartfelt discussion had commenced before bedtime, but not prayer. The next night was fraught with frustration and disappointment, and Sir Theo ran out of the bedroom and disappeared. Reba Jean waited a few moments, then went to hunt her husband. She was unsure if she should try to console him or leave him alone. She found him in his prayer closet, kneeling before God. She slipped her arms around him and held him close, and he began to pray aloud. They prayed together for some time and then both went to bed and tried to sleep. Reba Jean still wasn't sure what her husband had resolved, if anything.

The next morning, she overslept, but as she left for her weekly lecture, she was assured by Sir Theo that he was alright. It became a very strange morning. However, the afternoon was quiet, with some time to write. It had been a year since she wrote her first book and then had gone through the editing process. She was about to sync up with her editor this week to start the process with the second book. She really hoped to have the companion devotional finished by the middle of the month and submit that. She had re-read the entries she had written thus far, and they had really encouraged her yet again.

It was that time of night again. Would they pray together? Reba Jean finished writing and waited to see if her husband would lead them in prayer. A knot of stress formed in her stomach. This should be a wondrous time, so why did it feel like she was hanging onto a shred of hope every night?

Chapter 4

Reba Jean did not write anything for the next month. The discontentment had dissipated with a long week of rest. The anger was no longer a current issue, and she had resolved the conflict of whether God wanted her in the ministry that she had been thrust into.

The issue of whether what influences you also defines you was still very much in the forefront of her thoughts. She had been treasure collecting in sermons, lessons, social media posts, and hymns. She couldn't wait to express those treasured thoughts in her Treasure for the Heart devotional. The editor had let her have more room for each devotional entry so that she would hopefully expound a bit more about the precious treasure in the Word of God. However, they eventually both agreed that the length she was using was most suitable, as it was to be a devotional and not a Bible Study book.

The prayer time with Sir Theo was hit or miss; it seemed to depend on whether he had a pressing issue that he wanted to pray about with her. She still prayed inaudibly every night as they lay in bed together as if they were praying aloud. She found she slept better and was able to get up earlier when she went to bed and prayed before sleep. The mutant in the Library seemed to have gone into hibernation once they started praying together.

Reba Jean paused her fingers on the keyboard and listened to the hymns playing in the living room. She had read just that morning that music was a huge influence on us and a real treasure when it was about the Lord. The soft whine of the Velcro puppy interrupted her. She was praying it would be more independent of her; however, it seemed to only use its independence when Sir Theo was around. Reba Jean closed her eyes and rubbed her face. It had been a trying morning with the puppy clinging to her and the cats following her, the big dog barking, and the replay of a conflict unresolved ricocheting through her mind.

She had been thrust in the middle of a present-day Euodias and Syntche scenario. The two ladies were in agreement that there was a conflict, but both disagreed on how to resolve it. One was very dogmatic and self-justified, whilst the other wanted compassion and help with the issue. The issue was petty and hopefully would be temporary. However, being an empath as she was, it nagged at her whether she had given the right counsel to both of these women. That evening, the preacher even preached about fellowship and how necessary it was. She felt like all she was now going to be able to do was just pray for both of them to restore fellowship with each other.

There had been another thing that had bothered her the last few days, as well. She had been terribly convicted to go visit the new neighbors on either side of her and invite them to church or share Jesus with them. She really wanted to do this, but she was scared! She prayed for power, strength, and courage; she looked at those houses and just couldn't muster the courage to go do it. Earlier that day, she stood on the patio and resolved that she would take Sir Theo with her, and then she wouldn't have to be scared. She prayed about this issue and told God that she would do it with Sir Theo. Later in the afternoon, a vehicle pulled into the driveway. It was one of the new neighbors! She was able to invite them to church and children's ministries! God brought one of the neighbors to her own driveway! She managed to get the other neighbor to at least wave back at her from across the yard. She determined that she would go visit the other side as well, so that God didn't have to coax her. She was thankful, though, that He had removed that hindrance from her.

Now, she just needed the right words to say to the probable cultists that seemed to want to share their twisted interpretation of Scripture with her once a week. She had tripped them off their script a few times, but they got right back on it and did not even seem to hearken to what she said from Scripture. That was her cue that they were probably unidentified cultists. They had come back the next week, and Sir Theo met with them out in the drive, and they did not want to share Scripture with him, he said. Reba Jean found that intriguing, and it reminded her of the Scripture that warned of silly women being led astray… She felt like a target was on her to see if she could stand firm on the truth of God's Word. Oddly enough, they never returned, and her husband said they were probably intimidated by him.

Reba Jean soaked in the stillness of the Library; she had come up here to write, while the puppy chewed its bone. She did not know how long that bone would last, so she wanted to be a good steward of the time she was able to spend. Her eyes fastened upon the title of a book that was in front of her. It was entitled *Release the Power of Prayer.* "Wow! Now that looks interesting!" Reba Jean thought almost aloud. She had found many more Scriptures on the issues that she was feeling frustrated with, and she felt like she was armed and ready to overcome and conquer. She felt a heavy burden fall upon her as she thought of Lady Constance at that moment. The dogs began barking at the new neighbors, and she got distracted. However, she returned to the Library and, in the quiet, was about to pray when the phone rang. She really wanted to pray for Lady Constance but kept getting interrupted!

The phone call ended, and Reba Jean found herself distracted again. With a start, she realized that she still hadn't really prayed for Lady Constance, at least not as fervently as she had desired. The phone call had drawn her away from the Library, but with renewed intent, Reba Jean returned to the Library and knelt in prayer for her friend. Her earnest intercessions came to a satisfied end, and she was confident that the Lord would intercede for her friend in whatever this burden was about.

Reba Jean leaned back and let the atmosphere of the Library envelope her until another cat got in her face. She picked up the overly loving, curious feline and set it on the other side of her. It scampered off with the puppy, and she listened to the two cavort across the floor. Looking over to her other side, she saw another cat just watching them. She tamped down a sprig of anxiety as she realized it was another one of her own cats, not a minion. When did the Library become the zoo's playground?!

She felt something feathery brush her face, and as she wiped it away, she realized it was a tendril of thought. She looked at it and had her answer, the zoo had invaded her space because she let it! She exhaled deeply, trying not to be stressed or frustrated, and the exuding air blew away all the tendrils that had been poised in thought around her. That feeling of nausea returned, and she recognized it from weeks earlier. It had to be triggered by the zoo, so how could she defeat it? She looked in amazement as a page from a book floated down to the floor and a golden strand from the Ancient One began to write *FIND HELP IN THE BIBLE when you are facing*…and it began to list Scripture references for her to look up. She saw verse references about anxiety and crisis and figured they would probably suffice. This was a bit different because instead of the Ancient One flipping to the different references, It was going to make her look them up on her own instead.

Lady Constance sent a missive to her just as she was about to open the Ancient One to remind herself what Proverbs 3:7 said. Then Sir Theo came home, and she had to leave the Library. She felt thwarted at every turn, but she would persevere and look up that Scripture tonight! However, that did not happen. It wasn't until the next morning that she looked up Proverbs 3:7, and it just did not seem to apply in the category that the help sheet had listed it for. She read it a few times and then just decided to read the whole chapter. The whole chapter of Proverbs 3 was about getting wisdom and what a treasure and crown of glory it would be to the person who possessed it. That, of course, struck a chord with her and made her run to the Library to see if wisdom was in her treasure stash.

Reba Jean looked at her celestial cache and wondered how she could gauge what she actually had. She knew that it wasn't always quantity but probably more implementable quality that mattered when it came to the treasures for the heart. Some days she felt almost as if she had very little treasure gathered, and other times she felt robbed of what she had gathered. Her treasures from the celestial realm influenced her, but she felt like they needed to define her.

She looked up the meaning of the word "define" to see if it expounded further on her initial understanding of the word. Calling out to Lady Jane, she showed her the meaning of the word "define". They both looked up the word "influence" to see what that meant. They looked at each other as they mulled it over together.

"So, something that defines me, describes my nature and my being exactly, and something that influences me just affects that nature, but not necessarily in totality or exactly." Reba Jean summarized it, just as she had thought, nothing had changed in looking up the meanings that she had already known. However, she was very much aware that too many people let influences define them. Lady Jane looked pensive for a few moments, and she thoughtfully considered how she, too, thought that everything that happened to the Library defined it. She then realized that there were powerful influences, but the true definition of what the Library and she were to be was already delineated clearly in Scripture!

Over the next few weeks, Reba Jean spent much of her time working on, albeit mulling over, the influences in her life. When God directly told her to separate from a person, she obeyed, not knowing all the reasons, but still obeying. It was almost a surprise to her to feel the freedom that came when she did what God said for her to do. Oddly, it almost seemed to be an unwritten rule that obedience was a burden. She found it liberating, actually, to know she was doing God's will. The prayer closet issue was no longer an issue, and her heart cried out in gratitude. She had also totally put the whole ministry responsibility and weight into God's Hands. He had shown her His answer in her devotions that she had been appointed because of her faithfulness. The Bible was full of such divine appointments, so why did she think anything had changed with her unchanging God?

Chapter 5

Her husband took the puppy for the afternoon and gave her instructions to write! Thankfully, she was able to catch up on the entries for *Treasure for the Heart*.

However, just a day later, she was thrust into the middle of a family squabble, which showed her a vivid illustration of what she had just read in Esther 5. Who you surround yourself with will influence either side of your nature. Be around those who will always direct you to do what God desires. She realized that a majority of the men that she and her husband were surrounded with, albeit considered spiritual leaders, had a huge anger issue along with a distorted view of what their wives were to be.

After a long visit with Lady Matilda, she heard an echo of the same thought that her editor had voiced in their last meeting. When you see such anger and malice spew forth from someone, it's usually rooted in a deeper spiritual issue and not actually the supposed petty situation that caused the explosive reaction. Scripture upon Scripture ran through her mind as she mulled and prayed over this situation. These men KNEW the Bible, and yet they did not seem to adhere to it, as if it only applied to others. Lady Matilda and Lady Dana both suggested that insecurity or the feeling of not being in control or even their feeling of being inferior could make them react in such a manner.

Reba Jean knew that not all men were like this, so why did she seem surrounded by so many of them? Were they influencing each other to react in such a venomous way to their female loved ones? She looked up the meaning of influence and was shocked to see that the world equated it with power and manipulation. She knew books were written and became best sellers on how to influence people, but the idea of manipulating someone and having that power or control over them just seemed very scary to her.

She had begun reading that book called *Release the Power of Prayer* about George Muller, and he had stated that you should never let status influence you. Her mind immediately went to all the types of influences that were so prevalent: social influence, good or bad influence, etc. Even a widely-used social media platform uses the concept of "status" in its idea of sharing to influence the viewer. She rubbed her forehead in concern as she realized how much of her current socio-economic construct was built around "influence."

Reba Jean wondered if her question about influence versus defining was skewed. She had been so intent on looking for how God defined her based on Scripture, and yet everyone around her seemed bent on influence, not definition. No, she would not be swayed, she determined, as a verse, almost as if it had come from the Golden Words of the Library's Ancient One, came to mind. It said in Romans 12:3, *"For I say, through the grace given unto me, to every man that is among you, not to think of himself more highly than he ought to think; but to think soberly, according as God hath dealt to every man the measure of faith."* She had compared thinking to influence as if they were synonymous.

Reba Jean began to do a study on the word "influence;" in flow of an action or process seemed to be the simple breakdown of the word. However, the suffix "ence" denoted a feeling of extreme aversion or detestation, and she somehow felt as if that applied to the current affect or, should that be effect, this word had on her. After a bit more word study, she lapsed back into thinking about the family squabble and the person that God had told her to separate herself from. She swiftly realized

46

that these situations were affecting her mood and thus were controlling her thoughts!

Reba Jean decided to escape to the Library for a little while. She entered that lovely, mysterious place, and after securely fastening the door, she hastened to the Treasure Room. She hoped that by sitting amongst the treasures, she would begin to think about good things. Her cat, Mellow, had a royal conniption when he could not gain access to her. He frantically called for her and scratched at the door, purred like a lion, and created a fuss that even Sir Theo could not deter him from. Reba Jean did not want the zoo invading her space; she needed to think. The Library had been a place of secrets that had been exchanged for treasure, and now she wanted that treasure to influence her and others. If that was the case, then influence was not necessarily bad; it could be used for good. She did not want to manipulate, con, or control people; she just wanted them to let the power of God work in their lives and in their libraries.

Days turned into weeks as Reba Jean pondered the power of influence over people's minds and lives. She took a multitude of notes on scraps of paper and on her daily planner as she found Scripture during her study time that would be good to use for her books and devotionals. Lady Constance had influenced her to start a Bible study with Skye and her, as well as other study plans, both personally and collectively. Each day felt like she was being ripped down to the core as issues of anger, fear, patience, pride, and faith were explored and pored through. The introspection was nothing new to Reba Jean, but knowing that she needed to dig up the roots of her issues often put her at a loss as to what the actual root cause of these was.

Just today, she felt as if she might have figured out why the study guide had labeled her issues as fear and pride. She just wanted to be valued and loved but not to be puffed up and have a sense of power or entitlement. She needed to be careful that her… Reba Jean paused in her thoughts, tidied up her desk, and fiddled with the spacing of her desk items. She wasn't sure how to complete that thought. Was her needing to be loved, wanted, accepted, and cherished a matter of pride? This might not be a thought or question that could be so easily answered in a matter of seconds. Reba Jean shifted in her chair and decided to just shelf that thought to ponder over. It was odd that, as a burgeoning wordsmith, she often could not find the correct word to describe what she was thinking.

Peering over at her notes from the last three weeks of not writing felt almost overwhelming. A gnawing feeling started in her stomach, and she recognized it as stress. An unexpected job offer had been presented to her, one with no pressure, no family obligation, no "volun-told" aspects to it. She was free to truly seek God's will. It had been a precious time of getting close to God even though He had daily and sometimes hourly told her to "BE STILL, to wait on Him, to not lean on her own understanding." Reba Jean had done that, but she was still susceptible to the influence that her godly counselors had all given her.

Realizing that she was "languishing," as the Lady Matilda had called it, she was overthinking and letting her fear of doing something out of the will of God cloud her view of what this opportunity might have in store for her from God. It did answer the prayers of not having to do physical body-harming labor, and it kept her from having to be in the zoo. Lady Dana had reminded her that structure was probably more beneficial for her, and Sir Theo had seconded that. He knew that sometimes structure felt restrictive but that she could be more productive in every area of her life with a more structured day.

Reba Jean accepted the job offer and hoped for a fully settled sense of peace from the Lord. She did not get the feeling she expected, but even if God remained silent on the employment side, His presence was very real and close. He was very vocal about her lectures to the itinerant librarians and the myriad of Bible Studies that she was doing. Reba Jean paused as she could almost hear Lady Constance's voice singing clearly in her mind a song that they had re-written for themselves and shared with the young librarians. Reba Jean dug out a copy of the song; she was still trying to memorize it and decided to take it up to the Library to show Lady Jane.

Lady Jane felt the air change in the Library, and she went to see who had arrived. These days, it is often a surprise to see who ends up in the Library. The Lady Constance was a frequent visitor, and she had a sneaking suspicion that Sir Theo often stepped just inside to see what was going on. The mutant had reared its ugly head a few times and had run rampant through the Library only to be shoved back into its closet. Why the mutant was allowed to even stay anywhere near the Library was still a surprise to Lady Jane. The Lady Dana and the Lady Diane were gentle, soothing visitors who always left Lady Jane wishing they would stay longer.

As she entered the atrium, she saw Reba Jean wandering around in circles near the crystal Fountain, humming a tune. Lady Jane snickered to herself and tried not to giggle; she really hoped Reba Jean would not start singing. Catching herself with that less-than-gracious thought, she wondered where that had come from. Singing praises to King Abba was what helped them survive this last year. Why was she thinking such a critical thought now? Lady Jane gave herself a stern, mental shake and went to see what Reba Jean was humming.

"Lady Jane!" Reba Jean grasped her little avatar of the Library and showed her the wrinkled paper of printed words. Lady Jane recognized it now; it was the new version of "This Little Light of Mine," which had been reworked in a personal way.

> This little light of mine, Yes! I must let it shine,
> This little light of mine, Yes! I must let it shine,
> This little light of mine, Yes! I must let it shine;
> Let it shine, Let it shine, Let it shine.

The second verse was changed to: "Hide it under an angry mood, No! I must let it shine," and repeated in the same manner as the first. Then, Reba Jean and Lady Constance changed the next two verses as well to say, "Won't let my mind blow it out," followed by "Gonna shine it through my little house, I must let it shine."

Lady Jane found herself humming it as the tune was easy to get caught in her mind, even if the words were a bit harder to remember as they were changed from the version she had heard all her life in the Library. Two heads bobbed and weaved back and forth as they practiced the new words; however, there was a deep truth under the personal version that was not easily dismissed.

A few moments passed in this amenable manner until Reba Jean came to an abrupt stop and knew it was time to sit down and write. She wandered through the main Library shelves, pulled out a stack of loose papers and a couple of books, and wandered back to the desk that appeared seemingly out of nowhere any time it was needed. Reba Jean had not meant to cut Lady Jane off mid-note, but she had one of those multi-tracked minds, and the mental train had jumped the rails and was on another track already.

Just as she started to get organized, a muttering started and increased in volume. Reba Jean whirled around to see that Sir Theo's Library entrance was right behind her, and he was talking to himself and her. She looked around, disoriented; she had not thought that her desk was so close to Sir Theo's office before now. It was disconcerting how this Library always seemed to change size and shape, and you just never knew what was going to happen in here. Being so close to Sir Theo's office gave her a bit of anxiety; he would distract her, and she remembered how the hornets had come through his office. In fact, many of her issues seemed to be intertwined with his office, or was it with him?

A cat tiptoed past her, and she followed it. It turned around as she went back to her desk. It was just one of her own cats, coming to sleep in the Library. Reba Jean still did not like her zoo to be able to come into the Library, but, as of yet, she had found no real permanent solution. At least the puppy was with Sir Theo in his office! The fact that his office and her Library were connected and often seemed to be enveloped within each other was a conundrum that she did not want to delve into very deeply.

OK, it was time to get back to writing the devotional Treasure for the Heart! She wanted to be able to cover all the scribbles and notes that she had taken in the last three weeks and file those away. Then, she would be ready for the next time that God showed her more treasure in His Word! The cat distracted her again. She closed her eyes into slits and mentally willed it to just leave her alone.

Chapter 6

It had been so thrilling to catch up on her devotional entries over the last week. She had caught up on housework, did the new hire paperwork for the new job, and sneaked over to see the grandbaby a couple of times. She had even radically changed her hair and no longer resembled her mother. This change in appearance had really helped her disposition. Things should have been going well, but as her life was always a paragraph away from chaos, so it was even now.

With heavy steps and an even heavier heart, Reba Jean ascended the staircase to the Library. Without even letting the artifacts or golden strands from the Ancient One greet her or Lady Jane to distract her, she headed down the corridor of hope straight to the nursery. Once inside, the stale air of the closed-up room smothering her, she sank down on the bed and stared into nothingness. The room no longer looked like a nursery; it was part closet and part guest room, and all the baby stuff was stored in a corner. The kids had informed her and her hubby that they could only see the baby at a certain time of day with permission. The time slot they were allotted was, of course, during the working hours of their jobs. What had influenced them to react in such a way?

Reba Jean looked up as feathery, golden strands descended out of the ethereal and formed themselves into a beautiful golden-shaped baby. Reba Jean still had her last memory of snuggling her little grandbaby and feeling her snuggle her back. She had gone through the actual stages of grief as if she had lost her grandbaby. All she had was this memory to cherish. She looked around the room and decided that this would be her prayer closet up here in the Library. It matched the one down below, and she needed to have double the prayers going up.

Her brother had called her in the midst of all this, and he had declared that he would join his prayers with hers! She had felt as if a warrior had joined her ranks, and she could taste the victory! Sir Theo, however, had not reached her level of victory, so dealing with a very upset hubby was just as thwarting as defeating the enemy that had arisen. There was no doubt this was a spiritual battle, but God had reminded her to be strong in Him and in the power of HIS might! This could also be temporary, not necessarily long-term. Reba Jean curled up on the bed and began to pray in earnest for the kids and her little golden child.

Lady Jane had noticed Reba Jean heading down that corridor and, because she was, of course, the avatar of the Library who knew maybe even better than her mistress did as to what was going on, followed her quietly at a distance. Lady Jane heard the books rustling and felt the mutant wrestling against its confining chains, but knew that only Reba Jean could decide what would happen in the Library. When Reba Jean closed her eyes, it was not in defeat, and Lady Jane could feel the determination and purpose permeating the air around the former nursery. The beautiful, sweet savor of prayer soon flooded the room and covered them with celestial essence.

As her prayer drifted upward, she realized that she was not alone. Oh, she knew now that Lady Jane was in the room with her, but she was keenly aware that the Comforter had come!

Opening her eyes, she locked her gaze with Lady Jane, and they silently communicated their thoughts to each other. No books were opened or written in; only hearts and desires were expressed in silence.

Resolutely, Reba Jean intertwined her fingers with Lady Jane, and they meandered about the Library almost in a daze.

Feeling a tapping on her shoulder, Reba Jean found a book trying to get her attention. A misty tendril descended and formed into a long quill pen. Reba Jean looked at the title of the book. It had been entitled *Regrets*, but those letters had been burned off, and now it said… Well, it said nothing! There was no title… Reba Jean was not sure this book should be opened—or even written in. Lady Jane saw the book and the quill and had an odd feeling skitter up her spine.

Looking at each other and this suspicious book, the girls took the Golden Sword and slashed at the book. If it passed the test of the Golden Sword, they could re-title it and make it a good book. If it did not survive being divided asunder, then it could be thrown into a strong box and locked up for all eternity! The book shivered, the quill quivered, and the Golden Sword from the Ancient One sliced the book straight through. Shrill screams started and were abruptly silenced, and soon, it was apparent that this book would never be written in again!

Lady Jane grabbed some misty tendrils, formed them into a broom, and swept up the ashes of what was left of the Book formerly known as Regrets and locked them into a strong box. How many more books of regrets were lurking around the shelves in this conundrum of a Library? Together, they washed their hands in the Fountain of Living Water and felt the last vestiges of darkness vanish off of them.

Reba Jean went to her writing desk and opened the third book that she had been working on. It was about influences. She saw a note that she had left on her desk to include in her next entry. It said that whatever we place our hope in during difficult times is what influences our ability to cope. How applicable that note was right now! She had the corridor of hope, but she could not place her hope in a room or a hallway or in people. She could and would only place her hope in her Anchor, Jesus Christ! This situation did affect her, but it did not define her.

As she began to write, words from the Ancient One curled their way upon golden strands around her pen, and she felt the comfort come through Scripture that King Abba,

Himself, sent straight to her. Hearing another book trying to get her attention, she saw that it was her sermon notebook. It opened to the Sunday School lesson from the previous day. It read, "How am I acting? How do we react? This is what gets you out or keeps you in. Motivation isn't your influence what causes you to stop is the crucible." She pondered over that note; it had made sense when she wrote it, but now it seemed like she was missing a thought or word. Aha! It wasn't a word but a semicolon; she quickly inserted the semicolon, and now it made more sense to her. She giggled; her editor would probably roll her eyes at that note.

She glanced at a note about demonic influences; boy, she did not want to even delve into that thought right now. She picked up the note and filed it away in her desk. She did not know if she would ever elaborate on the influence of the Nether Realm. She shivered when she thought of Captain Insidious and General Nefarious. Just as quickly, she grabbed the Golden Sword just in case those thoughts were construed as an invitation to those demonic influencers.

Twirling around, ready for battle, all she saw was Lady Jane putting books back on shelves and swishing away dust motes. Exhaling, she realized she had been holding her breath, and her chest hurt from the fear. The Ancient One got her attention, and the golden words reminded her again to be strong in the Lord and in the power of His might! She relaxed but kept the Golden Sword in her hand.

Faintly, the strands of a violin could be heard from somewhere in the dark aisles of the numerous tomes. Reba Jean and Lady Jane looked at each other with some trepidation; this music sounded wild and heartbreaking. It did not remind them of the beautiful tones of praise from the music room, neither did it seem to emanate from that direction. Clasping hands together, each with a Golden Sword raised, they advanced towards the source of this eerie music. After walking through multiple rows of books whose titles remained darkened, they arrived in front of a little alcove.

There, a letter **V** sat playing a strange song on a violin. This might seem strange to anyone who did not have such a remarkable Library as they had. The **V** was sitting there, but it seemed to have strings attached to it, much like a marionette. Reba Jean raised her sword and violently slashed through the strings. With a screech, the **V** was disconnected from its puppet master and fell into a bunch of little 'v's' strewn at their feet. With the Golden Sword, Reba Jean touched first one **V** and then another; soon, the words vendetta, vengeance, vicious, vitriol, vent, vindication, and ventilate were all spelled out around them. They read each word to themselves; they were NOT going to voice these words into thoughts! By the time they got to the word "ventilate," neither of them felt like they could breathe... Wait-breathe! They needed to take a breath and not let these stages of grief overwhelm them. The Golden Swords rearranged the words, and soon, the passage from Romans 12 was written in golden letters on the floor instead. Vengeance belonged to the Lord; they needed to overcome evil with good! God had the victory; they just needed to stand in the power of His might.

Exhaling again and almost spent with relief, they both acknowledged that the Nether World had tried once again to defeat them. Fortunately, they both had the foresight and fortitude to bring their Golden Swords with them! Shaking their heads, they took the violin, and after dunking it in the Fountain of Living Water to cleanse it, they took it to the music room where it could only sing songs of Zion!

The next day, however, thoughts of the word "vindication" were still swirling around the outskirts of Reba Jean's mind. She reacted badly to her husband's bad reaction. Yes, that's how it seemed lately. The only way to get his attention concerning his bad behavior was to react in the same manner as he was acting. He apologized multiple times, but it took a while for Reba Jean to calm down. The day after, as she did her devotions, she meditated on the thought that it was possible that humans had so re-programmed their brains to only recognize their bad behavior when it was mirrored back to them. Scripture repeatedly showed Christians how they were to respond and behave, yet it seemed so futile when they were so blinded to the truth.

Reba Jean spent the morning meditating on her devotions; it had even included the passage about daughters-in-law turning against mothers-in-law. It also repeated in two separate devotionals the story of Martha versus Mary. Reba Jean keenly observed when something was repeated to her; she was left to ponder, though, was she being Martha or Mary?

Her thoughts were still swirling, and no real sense of peace reigning in her spirit or mind, so she decided to escape to the Library. The puppy started whining, and her husband kept fussing at it, but nothing changed. He finally scooped up the puppy; at least he was more aware of the nuisance that she was. Good. Maybe she could get to the Library without any of the zoo following her this time.

She looked around herself and had an interesting thought. She was in her husband's office, which mirrored his Library. Was it possible to gain entrance to her Library through his? She would not have to go back to the living room and ascend that staircase, as that just felt like it would be a very long climb for her. She slowly turned her head in every direction. How would she get to the Library from here?

In her Library, there was an archway, that dreaded connecting portal that had been such a heartbreaking site of destruction in recent months. She did not want to pass through that portal. The less it was used, the more secure it might stay. Glancing to her right, she spied a bookshelf. It caught her eye because the top shelf was full of HER books—her favorite tomes and the ones she had just published. With eyes widened in anticipation, she tiptoed to the bookshelf and eyed each title. A tingle of something yet unnamed raced down her spine. Each title felt like an event that had happened or might happen to her.

Which title opened the secret door to her Library? She was sure there was a secret entrance here; she just had to find it. She wanted to be so careful, though, as she had a feeling that each book was an entrance to different parts of the Library. With titles like *Submerged, Called to Die,* and *The Choice,* she had to be extremely careful which book she wanted to pull out as the hidden lever. Running her eyes over *Every Storm* and *The Long Road Home,* she came across the title *A Place Called Home.* Something settled in her spirit; she could have chosen *Castles* or *The Princess,* but she decided to see where this book would take her instead.

Slowly, Reba Jean pulled out the book entitled *A Place Called Home,* and the bookshelf moved just enough for her to slip in. Was she in her Library? It was dark at the moment, wherever she was. She sniffed the air. Birds could be heard chirping, and muted sounds from Sir Theo's Library could be faintly discerned. She smelled the stale, musty air of an unused chamber. Her eyes seemed to adjust to the lack of lighting, and in the silence, she felt an untenable calm settle upon her. It seemed to come from the chamber, not from inside of her.

The silence seemed to be even more noticeable; she could still hear Sir Theo's voice, and a deep sigh emanated from his office/Library. She turned almost in programmed response, thinking that she should go back. Instead, Reba Jean squared her shoulders. She wanted to be in a place called home, and if she could find that in her Library, then onward she must venture. Her eyes scanned the space in front of her. Soon, objects seemed to become visible: a baby's bib, her second book, a penny jar, and some bric-á -brac. Oh! These looked like items from her writing desk! Was she in the Library or at her writing desk?

Reba Jean remembered that many of the same rooms in her house were reflected in the Library. She could still feel the stale air, so she knew she wasn't downstairs. Inhaling and struggling to know what to do, she felt her chest clench with anxiety. She was going to hyperventilate and for no real reason! Ventilate, ah yes, that word that reminded her to "breathe." She exhaled with a lingering, measured breath and tried to gird her fortitude together.

She exhaled one more time, then ventured forth into the possible unknown. Rounding a corner, there was the Library all laid out before her, its vast expanse of books displayed as far as she could see.

She wondered if this was the place called home. She twisted her expression into something akin to a grimace and began walking through the aisles of tomes. What had she expected? She felt almost disappointed that she was in her Library! The very place she had been trying to get to from her husband's office!

That book title had somehow given her other thoughts—intangible feelings of longing. She did not want to be in her home, or even in a place called home; she wanted to FEEL at home. A place of peace, calm, love, and acceptance. A nurturing place where she could grow and feel like she belonged.

That was what she had secretly expected when she pulled that book out; she had hoped to escape to a different reality! She was not comfortable in her own skin; she felt unsettled in her own home. No wonder she was looking for something else.

She shuffled along the aisles, not even looking at the books or where she was going. Plodding along, lost in melancholy, she bumped into something or someone. Lifting her head, she saw she had collided with Lady Jane. Lady Jane looked at her with a myriad of emotions flitting across her face. Perplexed at her mistress' mood, Lady Jane decided not to voice her thoughts. Instead, she wrapped an arm around her mistress and began walking with her, matching plodding step to plodding step.

Reba Jean acknowledged her avatar's presence—partially welcomed it, partially resented it. She wanted to shrug off that beautiful arm, wanted to lash out at her or start crying. Tears began to slide down her cheeks as the gamut of emotions raced through her. Lady Jane slightly tightened her loving hold on her mistress and wondered where they were going and whether she should direct their steps to the Ancient One.

What seemed like hours later, even though it was really just seconds, Reba Jean stopped in her tracks. Lady Jane almost stumbled when they came to such an abrupt halt. Reba Jean's eyes darted back and forth, and her face had a strange expression on it.

"Did you hear that?" Reba Jean asked Lady Jane.

Now, Lady Jane schooled her expression into one of calm and decided not to outwardly react. This was the Library, after all; you could hear all sorts of things in here, and how you reacted could create any number of potential disasters!

Reba Jean strained her ears. Yes, she was hearing voices, more like whispers! Cocking her head to the side, she practically dragged Lady Jane along as she began following the sound of those whispers. Lady Jane wanted to panic; surely, this was NOT a good idea. She wanted to jerk herself out of Reba Jean's grasp and bolt like a scared deer back to her safe place in the portico of peace. Reba Jean strode onward as if on a mission—or the warpath. Lady Jane was not sure which intent her mistress had in mind.

They rounded a bend in a corridor that they had not remembered seeing before and nearly fell into the yawning maw of a round chasm. What was this? Whispers could be heard rising up through the mist in the expanse. Reba Jean sat down on the edge, and then lying down she put her head over the opening to better hear the whispers.

"It's a Whispering Well," declared Lady Jane to her mistress.

Reba Jean countered with, "No, I think it's an echo chamber."

It was technically both; the whispers were echoes of voices that Reba Jean had heard and listened to recently. She could hear Lady Matilda, Lady Constance, and Lady Dana more predominantly. Reba Jean listened and remembered conversations; most had been concerning the situation with the children. Each one had family members who had been influenced to serve themselves or the world and to run from God.

61

Reba Jean was not alone. The voices were the voices of influence that she surrounded herself with. Currently, the voices brought help, hope, and comfort. She wanted to be careful that this echo chamber only whispered godly influences back to her. She could seriously envision this well being filled with all the "**V**" words if she was not careful.

Reba Jean spent some time listening again to the echoes of the whispers that were influencing her to stay close to Lord Rabboni and to just bask in His help and hope. Her idea of home, along with her reality of home, was probably a mixture of what not only influenced her but also what she chose to do with those influences. Lady Jane was a bit concerned about yet another new chamber in the Library, but it did not seem to have any danger attached to it currently. They dangled their feet over the edge, listening to the whispers; it was like an audible walk down memory lane.

After an undetermined stretch of time, the two companions rose to their feet, embraced each other, and walked back the way they had come. Reba Jean began thinking about the artifacts, the devotional she was in the middle of writing about the treasures, and slowly, a canopy of peace seemed to descend upon her and her avatar. This could have been a very dangerous exploration ending in a dark catastrophe, but thanks be to King Abba, it was not.

Reba Jean wanted to write more in the devotional *Treasure for the Heart*, but that had to come through Lord Rabboni, and she was waiting for content and context to go with the next few entry titles she had been given. She could, however, review Philippians 4:8, which was the current text she was using for her entries. She had written an entry for each of the eight things she was to be thinking about. She had made it to *things of good report* and seemed to hit a standstill. Maybe by studying what it meant to be of good report she would get the context of not only what it meant, but how to write about it. This was not just a devotional to write; it was a way to think and live and she was determined to institute its precepts and principles in her own thought life.

A short time later, Reba Jean sat back, stunned. She had written the devotional on things of good report and had read a good sermon from Spurgeon. A missive from the Lady Constance had her thinking more about Mary and Martha—a recurring theme that was inserting itself in her thoughts today. She decided to move on to things of virtue and looked up a lecture that she had given for the young librarians a couple of years earlier. On the second page of her notes, was yet again the story of Mary and Martha with Jesus at their house. What was God trying to tell her from this? It was no accident that everywhere she turned today, she was reminded about Martha and her busyness and Mary and her meditating on the words of Jesus.

Reba Jean did not start the devotional entry on virtue yet; she needed to find out what this business with Martha and Mary was all about first. She was listening but not getting any clarification, but God sure did have her attention. Oh, wait, maybe that was what this was really about! Was she really paying attention to Him, or was she too busy worrying about her family and petty, temporal things? Hmm, this would bear some further thought, so Reba Jean went out to the porch swing to ponder.

Reba Jean pondered for a few short minutes and decided to call Lady Constance. She shared with her how the recurring story of Mary and Martha was constantly being thrust at her. Lady Constance shared how that reminded her of a devotional she had bought but never really read. She mentioned the author, and Reba Jean leaped to her feet. On page one of the lecture notes, there was a note about a devotional by the same author! What was this? Lady Constance and Reba Jean talked over and excitedly, their words jumbled into each other. This lecture had been a few years ago; Reba Jean did not recall this devotional, nor could she find a copy of it in her possession. Yet, clearly, as noted on her lecture notes, she had seen it or referred to it over two years ago!

Reba Jean and Lady Constance excitedly discussed this and decided to do the devotional together! Sir Theo ordered the book for her and told her to repay the small amount owed in kisses. He was trying really hard today to be sweet.

Was this then the answer to why all these mentions of Mary and Martha were happening? It seemed so. Somehow, even years ago, God knew that she needed to do this devotional again, or for the first time. Reba Jean did not start on the devotional entry about virtue. She had a feeling that she needed to let this simmer until she started reading more about Mary and Martha. Lady Constance declared that if something was said tonight at church concerning this, she would probably verbally erupt.

In the middle of all this confabbing, Reba Jean got the notice that she would be starting her new job on Monday. She fought the slight sense of panic. Anxiety seemed to always be her first reaction. Lady Dana had reminded her a few weeks ago that this job was probably a good solution to her current issues, and yet she had a penchant for being anxious about anything and everything. She reminded herself and Lady Constance that she was to be anxious for nothing but in everything by prayer and supplication with thanksgiving to let her requests be made known unto God. She knew she would have His peace when she stopped being a worrier and started to be a warrior.

Chapter 7

Her first week of work was over, thankfully! Reba Jean was questioning everything about her life. The zoo and the previous physical job seemed tame compared to the week she had had. She was already begging God to let her stay home again. The synopsis from her sphere of influence seemed to state that this was to be expected, to just suck it up and keep moving. Her husband said this might be her desert place to draw close to God, encourage others, etc., listing various Biblical examples of desert places. Another devotional that she was reading made it seem like it was just a piece of a puzzle and that the whole picture would be revealed later when it was completed.

Lady Constance had been working on devotionals with her in the last month. Recently, they bought a book and began reading a section a day and discussing it together. It was about Mary and Martha. Reba Jean was a combination of both women, depending on the circumstance. She, however, was deeply concerned that this new job would make her become more of a Martha now.

Reba Jean was also studying a book on prayer by D.L. Moody, and it was in the section about forgiveness. Reba Jean had been fighting vindication for a while, and when her husband got a bout of poison oak, she found herself feeling vindicated often. He finally got to see what it was like. She knew it was not Christ-like; she fought it, but daily, she had to ask God to forgive her for liking the fact that he got to see what it was like. The circumstances of the outbreak were different, but the result was basically the same. She knew she wasn't to get satisfaction from him getting a taste of his own medicine, but it sure was a battle.

This forgiveness stuff was, however, very imperative, so she forgave her children for the hurt they caused through their selfish, sinful ways. She had been reminded not to brutally beat them over their heads for their wrongs but to just graciously, mercifully forgive them. She saw how she had a habit of wanting vengeance for being wronged, even if it was justifiable. Reba Jean reached out and opened the lines of communication again.

Next week was VBS. She was again in her place of supervision over her usual area of responsibility. She was already praying that she could lecture, work, supervise, and survive with her testimony intact. Reba Jean paused in her writing and decided she needed to visit the Library. She wanted to see if this week at a new job had caused any issues up there. She would not be surprised if Lady Jane was hiding again. It had been a rough week down here. Was the damage up there just as extensive?

Weary feet doggedly climbed the staircase to the Library. Fatigue seemed to billow out of the door as she pulled it open… wait, what? Did not the door usually open inward to the Library? Reba Jean stood with the door handle in her hand and studied the matter. Stupefied, she closed the door and then reopened it. Each time, she had to pull it open instead of push it open. She was baffled; surely, all the other times, it had not been this way. What was the significance of this? Shrugging finally, she entered the Library and then looked back at the door as she shut it. She slanted her eyes, and her face was drawn into a grimace with the confusion she still felt.

Reba Jean entered the vast interior of the Library almost as if it was foreign to her. She could hear Sir Theo talking in his Library; "curiouser and curiouser" drifted down to her ears. That completely described what she was thinking! Glancing around, everything seemed in its correct place. A long aisle of books, however, looked like a hurricane had stormed through them. She wandered over to see if she could clean up the mess or at least straighten it. The first few books slid back on the shelf easily; some of the others felt really heavy and didn't seem to want to go back on the shelf from whence they had surely fallen. She eyed the titles of these heavy tomes, wondering if they needed to be relocated.

Squinting in the dim light, she pondered over some of these titles. They did not really seem to disclose what was written inside. Was it safe to open these tomes and read them? She held a heavy tome next to her heart and felt anxiety arise within her chest. Her eyes widened, and she dropped the book with a crash. With bated breath, she tested each of the books on the floor this way. If she had any adverse reaction to just holding the book, she would drop it in the pile on the floor. If she was not sure, she put it in another pile to be tested further. The end of the aisle was finally reached, and she felt very unsettled. Anxiety was cutting off her breathing; surely, this was not a good thing. She needed to secure these books; they did not need to be opened if just touching them raised the hair on the back of her neck!

Reba Jean walked over to the Ancient One, picked up the Golden Sword, and, with a stern look in her eye, walked back to the first pile. With a "HIYAAAAH!" she brought down the Golden Sword as hard as she could onto the pile of books that had caused her severe emotional reactions. She did not know what to expect, but these days, the Golden Sword that represented the Word of God was her constant weapon. The Golden Sword cut through the entire pile of books, burning the paper within to ash. Golden tendrils reached out and swept up all the ashes into a pile, and with the help of the misty tendrils that were always dangling as well, she swept the ashen remains into a strongbox and locked it tight.

Approaching the ambivalent pile of remaining books, she took them to the Fountain of Living Water and dampened the hem of her skirt. Thus, she gently wiped them with her dampened skirt. If they sizzled or in any way reacted adversely, she would set them down on the Golden Sword. If they did not react adversely, she returned them to the shelf from whence they had originally fallen. This whole process might have taken a long time, yet because time was a wonky thing in the Library, it seemed to happen within minutes.

Reba Jean realized that now the shelves had plenty of bare spots to be filled with hopefully better books recording her thoughts in the future. Rubbing the back of her neck, she glanced around keenly, wondering if the tempest had only damaged this one row. The tempest might actually have been necessary because it showed her all the books that needed to be banished. These were the recordings of how she had thought and reacted sinfully during the many times that life had not gone how she had hoped or expected.

Walking around, she spied the manuscript of the devotional book she was writing, and emblazoned on the notepad next to it was the inscription, **The Just Shall Live By Faith!** Picking up the rest of her notes, she saw again the comment that she had noted from Charles Finney stating that if everyone used and lived the principles of the Gospel, what an immense influence they would have on the world. She pondered that again. Had she used and lived the Gospel in front of her new co-workers this last week? Had her being there been a good influence on them?

Lady Jane was sitting in the corner of the Library reading a book, giggling often and snickering in places. She heard Reba Jean come in, and some sort of kerfuffle had commenced, as usual. Meandering slowly towards her mistress with her nose in the book, she finally glanced up to see what Reba Jean was doing this time to the Library. All seemed quiet by the time Lady Jane arrived, and she wondered what the chaotic sounds had been just a few moments earlier. Reba Jean eyed the book in her hand suspiciously, and Lady Jane almost jerked with the intensity in her eyes. She found herself wanting to hide the book almost guiltily behind her back. Instead, she closed it with a misty tendril popping in like a bookmark to hold her place. With almost defiance, she brought it to her chest and looked defiantly back at Reba Jean. A peculiar battle of wills commenced all within the locked gazes of the two women. Simultaneously, they both slumped their shoulders in defeat. Halfheartedly, they gave each other a reluctant hug, almost shallow and superficial. Both of them despised these sorts of hugs, and yet here they were, subjecting the other to that very thing.

Both women flopped on the floor next to each other silently. Lady Jane reluctantly handed the book to Reba Jean. It popped open to where the misty tendril had been wiggling, and Reba Jean read words that had recorded the funny things that had been said or done in the last week. She, too, giggled when she read how the Lady Matilda had brought her two pounds of butter to show her just what the loss of two pounds of fat looked like. Reba Jean and Lady Jane snickered again; this book was really the other half of the happenings this week. It had only recorded the good things, and so it was worth keeping, even worth reading back through. Perspective and Perception were both keys in how to view situations.

Lady Jane pulled a cookie out of her pocket and began to nibble on it; she wondered if Reba Jean would gain back those two pounds just by looking at this cookie. She giggled at the thought, then ducked her head. She knew that Reba Jean really was trying to lose weight. However, food was a comfort to her, and boy, had this last week been one for needing comforting!

It was time to write again; every Saturday since she began her new job, she set aside part of that day to write. Would she be able to write in the devotional? She was trying to wrap her mind around the definitions of virtue. It was her next topic, and she had been meditating on it all week, actually longer. She could write about VBS, which had just finished; the highlight was the seventeen young precious professions of faith. A majority of those had been teenagers! She could talk about how she had run her big mouth too much, being too honest about how she felt about people. Would she mention how her husband finally saw all that she dealt with every year and how he was frustrated and discouraged by the human element that seemed to permeate their brethren?

Truth be told, she did not want to dwell on it either; she just prayed about it every time it came to her mind. She had made the weekly text to her daughter-in-law just to try to keep the lines of communication open at least once a week. The kids could run from her and God, but her prayers would chase them all the way back to Heaven! Reba Jean paused in thought and glanced at her notes. Were these notes for future devotionals, lectures, or writing in her novel? She saw another page of notes and remembered that she was going to write about the different influences of people, as found in the Scriptures.

Instead, she began fiddling with the pile of stuff on her desk. She always seemed to work better once she had it organized. Her husband had bought her a new iPad, and she had not even finished setting that up, so that was another thing that needed to be organized and completed. He had also purchased some devotionals for her at her request. She eyed them, trying to decide if they should stay on her desk or go on the bookshelf.

Her new iPad dinged. She opened the lovely blue butterfly cover that she had selected and cleared all notifications. She caressed the cover, and it brought her comfort. Making short work of her desk clutter, she wrote down the title for the devotional on virtue. Maybe, like the others, it would come to her as she wrote it. So many times, what she wrote often changed as it was put down compared to how she imagined it. Currently, she had thirty-eight devotional entries written and five more left to write before her list of ideas was used up again. God seemed to give her titles and thoughts in multiple batches, often during Sunday school or church.

Did any other Christian writers get inspiration from church services? She also got inspiration from her daily talks with Lady Constance or the devotionals that they studied together. Reba Jean typed a bit more in her novel and then went back to studying virtue. She was really intrigued by its various definitions and usage through time and wanted to dig deeper into it.

She saved the work on her novel and decided to open up the other manuscript and see how far she was able to delve into the mysterious merits of virtue. Just as she started typing, a severe thunderstorm whipped up, and she had to turn off her computer just to be safe. She kept the big dog company inside and then outside as the storm blew over so fast. The only sign of it was all the rain it had brought. She came back in to check on the mint harvest that she was drying. She set some aside for Lady Matilda, then started a late supper for her husband. He was working long hours this weekend, and along with VBS, their usual schedule was completely out of sync.

The house smelled of mint; it was soothing to her but a bit jolting to her husband. She laughed to herself inwardly at how opposite they seemed to be in nearly everything. Her husband called her over to look at a video he had taken of a teen activity during VBS. He was laughing at his commentary of it. It was good to hear him laugh after all the venting he had done previously about the self-centered adults. She could hear supper sizzling on the stove and decided to take a break yet again from writing. At least she had tried to write today. She took that as progress and refused to let the lack of quantity influence her mood.

After serving her husband his supper, she put the cats down for the night. The puppy thought it was bedtime; it would have been if this had been their usual schedule. She would finish this batch of mint in the oven, and then it would be time to shower after working in the garden all day and outside. Her mood was fairly calm and settled after such an arduous week both at work and church. She really missed being at home, and her husband had reassured her that she did not need to work.

After some bodily reactions to the stress, she almost quit her job just after starting it. However, she had prayed and listened to her hymn music and stayed in her Bible, and all of this seemed to help her finish the week of work with no further issues. The Scripture that she had been rehearsing in her mind was "none of these things move me" or something to that effect. She had even come up with a three-point outline today when she was telling Lady Constance about it. She knew it would turn into a lecture for the librarians at some point and be included in *Porch Ponderings*.

Reba Jean continued to reflect on her past week. She decided it was time to just stop stewing about the past week; she could not change what had happened or what she had said or done. However, she did try to sternly remind herself to behave better and be more Christ-like.

As she finished up her little projects for the night, she thought about one of their home improvement projects that had been assessed by a professional who advised against it. He recommended some possible upgrades to the current situation, but that was not necessarily an immediate need. She was disappointed that it was not really fixed but relieved that it would not cost thousands of dollars as she had expected it to. The point of her working was to be able to get out of debt faster and to help with home improvement projects. She found it interesting that some of these projects were turning into little things or nothing at all. She wondered again if she was to be working this new job at all.

That very question plagued her for the first month of her new job. Had she overstepped God's perfect will for her life? Repeatedly, the word "opportunity" was whispered to her, just like the words "Be Still" and "Unmovable" had permeated her very soul. The goal for this new job was an opportunity to get out of debt, sure, but it was more about being a witness and, above all, learning to trust God. This job required a level of trust that she hadn't needed in a while.

Reba Jean settled down to live her new normal, learning to trust God and to stop being so anxious. Her study on this subject was extensive and fruitful. She may not get to write as much or even study the Bible at leisure, but she found that her mornings and Saturdays were more precious. Her husband recognized these as treasures for both of them. This realization was an answer to a prayer that she had not realized had arrived after all this time. Hallelujah!

Chapter 8

Whispers from the well echoed through the corridors of the Library. What sort of whispering was this all about? Lady Jane had not seen much of Reba Jean in the last month; she had been consumed with her new job. However, the effect on the Library was noticeable. The books were often opened; usually, though, it was the Ancient One and devotional books. This was reassuring! The golden dust motes often wrote words in the air that seemed to control the atmosphere, keeping it stable.

It was Saturday, a day for Reba Jean to normally visit the Library. Would she appear at this later hour? Lady Jane wanted her mistress to go with her to the Whispering Well; she did not want to go alone. She watched a book drift towards her with a mysterious air. She caught it and looked at what had just been written in it a few moments before in the living room. Her eyes widened as she saw two pages of notes that Reba Jean had compiled on the "J" books of the Bible. It even had notes that Sir Theo had suggested! Lady Jane gave a half skip of happiness; her mistress might not have been here, but at least the living room was in good hands!

Reba Jean leaned back in her chair while her phone dinged off notifications faster than the speed of sound. Her daily at-length studies and fellowship with Lady Constance were such a blessing to her. Lady Diane had not been available since her return from her African missionary trip. Lady Constance, however, was living up to her name, constant! What a wonderful influence their journeys through Scripture were to them both.

This sphere of influence reminded her of the stories in the Bible of Job and his well-meaning three friends. Then there was Amnon and his wicked friend, who influenced him to commit evil and served as a warning to all to be careful who you listen to. Felix also came to mind. He listened to the Apostle Paul for years, and the influence was strong; he was almost persuaded to become a Christian but would not commit. Jesus had three close friends, but when He needed them most, they fell asleep. She was afraid she would have done the same, or she would have gone along with the crowd crying to crucify Him! The crowd mentality, the mob mentality was so prevalent in her current society.

Influence was so strong, yet it did not negate our free will or our command to obey Christ. Reba Jean remembered how the Library now contained a Whispering Well. She wasn't sure if it had always been there or if it appeared because of her recent desire to grow in the Lord. It had appeared as a barometer of what or who she was listening to. The urge to go see this well had Reba Jean bounding up the stairs to the Library. She yanked open the door determinedly, just in case it wanted to be ornery.

Inside the Library, the air was full of expectation and smelled like celestial incense. Her shoulders settled from a subconscious air of caution. She saw Lady Jane looking at a new book and smiling. This would surely be a good day in the Library after all! Reba Jean joined Lady Jane and saw the book was her study on the twelve "J" books of the Bible from that morning. They hugged each other, and then, with only their eyes, they communicated their unspoken thoughts. Grasping hands, they walked to the Whispering Well, passing by the corridor of hope. Reba Jean just shook her head, prayed silently as they passed, and continued with her avatar.

The whispers increased in volume and length as they neared the spherical chasm in the floor. Whispers of devotional titles with their thoughts, wondering about the kids along with prayers for them, victories over anxiety and concerns along with Scripture seemed to be the loudest. They sat down and dangled their feet over the edge, listening to see what else they could hear. Off to one side, they heard a muttering; leaning closer to make out what it was about, they felt like they were about to be pulled in! Gripping each other, they struggled for balance. The mutterings were about how annoying people were and how immature they had been acting. Most of the "people" were extended family or jobs.

The two girls looked at each other. Was all the spiritual stuff only on the surface and the lower levels were filled with wicked thoughts? Reba Jean narrowed her gaze, and a gleam of determination glinted from her azure eyes. Lady Jane felt panic at that look. She knew that Reba Jean was about to hurl down into the middle of that well! Was she going to go along or fight to stay safe? Would it matter either way? Reba Jean took a deep breath as if she was going to dive into a deep well of water. She took one last look at Lady Jane and left the decision up to her. She needed to see what was going on in the deeper recesses of her sphere of influence.

Thankfully, this well wasn't full of actual water; Reba Jean couldn't swim to save her life! She expected to go hurling down for miles, deep into the past. When she dived in, more like a lame duck than a swan, she did not expect to hit bottom so quickly. She stood up and could see Lady Jane's fearful visage a few feet above her. She thought about telling her to come on in the water was warm, but there was no water. Wait! It's a dry well. Should not there be the water of the Word in here? That ought to flush out any wicked whispers. The pun of her thoughts was not lost on her. She thought in analogies and puns all the time.

Surveying the wall of the well, she saw various stones with words on them. Her eyes widened in understanding; these stones were doorways to corridors beyond the well's interior.

She could explore the influences that were behind any of these stones if she dared. Looking around, she felt her skin crawl at some of the suggestions. She was thankful that the stones blocked the openings, but she was not happy that the influences of that sort lurked beyond.

Reba Jean did not want Lady Jane to see what types of influences were available in this well. She did, however, decide to drown out those voices, literally. Closing her eyes, she pictured the Fountain of Living Waters in the atrium of the Library. With the help of the misty tendrils and the golden dust motes, soon water from the fountain was being poured into the seemingly empty well. Reba Jean knew she wouldn't drown or die from being immersed in the Word of God. It simply floated her to the top of the well, where she could climb out.

Trembling from her discovery, she did not speak for a while. Lady Jane was worried but glad that there did not seem to be any immediate danger to them. She had not seen what her mistress had seen, so she did not really know how to react. Reba Jean thought about her mini escapade into the sphere of influence, the Whispering Well. Turning her head, she listened to see if the Living Water had changed any of those mutterings or drowned them out. With relief, she couldn't discern them now. She would need to watch the level of water and not let the well go dry.

Yanking on a few misty tendrils, she designed a stern sign that she posted on the rim of the well. "No Trespassing, Fishing, or Diving. Just keep OUT!" Lady Jane jerked her head back as if her mistress had struck her. Was this for her?! Lady Jane's ire began to rankle, but the touch of Reba Jean's hand settled her down. This sign was for both of them, along with any visitors, welcome or unwelcome!

Reba Jean, with trembling hands, turned away from the Whispering Well. She had enough of the sphere of influence for today. She needed to get back to writing about treasures for the heart instead! With that thought in mind, she dropped Lady Jane's hand and went off to find her writing desk and notes. She had a little time before she had to go practice being a good influence on others. She had a feeling it was these voices she had heard muttering, so immersing herself in the treasures of God's Word surely would help her have a better mindset.

The next few weeks brought this whole issue of influences shaping our minds and lives into vivid view. Her father ended up in the hospital with some serious health issues, and watching how he acted and reacted to various situations was a real eye-opener. She had tried to shrug off and bury the secrets of the past. Her husband was worried about all the triggers that being around her parents would activate. They sure did. However, she was shocked to realize that her father was not the shining hero but part of the trauma that she had blamed forever on her maternal figure. It was heart-rending to realize that her white knight, her rescuer, was just as culpable, and his feet were made of clay. It felt like utter betrayal.

Looking back, as unwillingly as she was to unlock that hurt and pain, she saw from the eyes of an adult what she had missed or ignored in her childhood of trauma. Her mother definitely had mental issues, but so did her father! She began to realize that it wasn't just the influence of her mother but deep-rooted issues in his own mind and life.

Reba Jean did what she could to honor her father, even at the risk of her mental health, but she found closure in the pain, if that was possible. She could not change her childhood, but she could change any learned behavior that was not glorifying to God. Influences were hugely evident in one's behavior patterns. Keenly aware of this, especially with her treasure hunt for spiritual jewels, she knew it was no coincidence that this dive into the secrets of the past had occurred. God had allowed this, her trauma, her struggle to make sense of it, to mold her, to polish her into what He wanted for her life.

It was difficult to put all her thoughts into words and to make sense of them, but she would try to write about them. Writing was therapy, just as talking with Lady Diane each week. Reba Jean had rehearsed all that she would say in her book through her thoughts during the days surrounding this. Yet, when the time came to sit down and try to put all those thoughts on paper, she found that she did not want to hash it all out yet again. If she had found closure, then maybe it needed to be case closed until something else re-opened the wounds of the past.

Devotional time each day was her oasis in the midst of all the voices trying to influence her. The repeating words "opportunity" and "immovable" still reverberated almost daily. She did not want to work, that much was true; she missed her time of writing whenever the muse struck. However, she knew that she must use this time of opportunity to witness for the Lord. She had wrestled often with this, and God had reminded her that she might just be sowing the seed. She may not see who watered as long as He got the increase. She could not, nor should she try to gauge her effectiveness upon results. She just needed to live and speak His Word and be a godly example for Him. What He chose to do with that was up to Him!

Lady Constance also stayed super busy and bemoaned that they no longer had time to study their devotional together or discuss what they were learning. Reba Jean threw that voice of influence up to the celestial realm as if to excuse herself from working such long hours. The answer that came back down to her again was "opportunity." She knew that for whatever time this lasted, she was where she was supposed to be, even if that meant shorter discussion times, relegated writing hours, and structured schedules.

Reba Jean was acutely aware of the 'watchers' as she called them. Two young ladies who loved her books and loved her and keenly watched everything she did. Skye and Daisy Mae were precious, but would they learn to hunt for spiritual treasure, or would she be found with feet of clay to them as well? She had a realm of influence, even if she felt she was a nobody.

Her realm of influence was vastly enlarged when one of her lectures was used for a large Sunday school class. Her eyes grew large at the thought of it. God had given her these thoughts to use in her lectures, and so far, one had gone out on the radio airwaves around the world, and another had just been used in Sunday school.

She felt a gamut of emotions and struggled a bit with fear. She wanted to be used like this for God's glory, but she wanted to stay humble. Using a pseudonym greatly helped with this. The majority of people did not know that she was an author. The lectures were thus useful when not colored by who wrote them. She knew that the small circle of people who were aware of her identity wanted to broadcast it far and wide. She always fiercely tamped down their urges. She wanted her writing to be all about the Lord and not her name or reputation, or lack thereof.

Reba Jean thought she was about halfway finished writing her third book, and she had hoped to be halfway finished with her first devotional. Opening her manuscript, she did a few mental calculations; she was not as far along as she had thought. She had a feeling that all the writing she did in her head each day had made her think that she would be pages and chapters ahead by now.

A thought struck her: what if... She stopped to explore that thought. It was a wisp of something, and she wanted to tug at it. Reba Jean ran up to the Library, where she could visualize this even better. Bursting through the door, she ran down the aisles, looking for that wisp of a tendril that she knew would be waiting for her to actually tug on it. Ah, there it was; it fairly quivered in anticipation. Should she really tug on this misty tendril of thought and see what it held? Glancing around just to assess if anything felt off or dangerous, Reba Jean threw off caution and tugged that wisp of a thought. Pulling the cascade of thoughts that tumbled out of the ether to her, she gathered them in her arms and placed them on the floor to see if she could make sense of them.

What if her actual trauma was still in a lock box, and all of these feelings were influenced by her siblings, who probably had not locked away their childhood trauma? She moved some of the wiggly thoughts around and wondered if that was an accurate assessment. She had talked daily with her brothers and sister and had hashed and rehashed things so much. She had gotten their pained perspectives, and it had influenced her. Her brother (Joe Nathan) and her sister (RaeAnne) were still dealing with their choices based on the influence of their trauma. Were they all stronger for it? Was their hashing these things over and all their questions actually helping them?

Lady Jane had seen her mistress dash through the aisles, and she felt unsure if she should be involved in whatever escapade this would result in. Then, she realized it was futile. She was curious; this was her Library, and that was her mistress. She was inevitably going to be involved. With a soft tread, she sidled closer to see what was going on. She was reluctant to make her presence known. Watching Reba Jean move wiggly tendrils around on the floor looked a bit odd, and she sat back to watch. She wondered if this is how Skye and Daisy Mae often looked as they, too, watched Reba Jean.

Reba Jean sat still with her hand still holding the misty tendril that she had tugged from the ether. It wiggled and pulsated but did not try to escape her grasp. It was as if it wanted her to feel every thought and nuance before being released back into the loftiness of the Library. Expressions of puzzlement, bewilderment, and thoughtfulness paraded across her features. With a sudden jerk, she let the tendril spring back into its usual residing place. A thought had so firmly pierced her heart that she almost thought the Golden Sword from the Ancient One had struck her.

Lady Jane saw her mistress jerk, the squiggly tendrils disappear, and a look of resoluteness settle her features. Reba Jean appeared to become stronger and more victorious even though she still sat there on the floor in the middle of an aisle. Lady Jane, with widened eyes, gulped, and this slight movement alerted Reba Jean to her presence. Her face swiveled in that direction, and the golden glint that came from her azure eyes almost blinded Lady Jane!

Reba Jean knew she needed to explain what she had just learned; it would be necessary for her avatar to utilize this as well. She opened her mouth to explain, then closed it just as emphatically. Jumping to her feet, she grabbed Lady Jane's hand and practically dragged her to the Ancient One. Lady Jane scrambled to keep her feet under her so that she would not be dragged like a sack of potatoes across the floor. They arrived at the Ancient One and found its shining pages poised in anticipation. It did not flip to the places that were racing through Reba Jean's heart and head; no, it waited for her to search for them.

"Serving the Lord with all humility of mind, and with many tears, and temptations, which befell me by the lying in wait of the Jews: And how I kept back nothing that was profitable unto you, but have shewed you, and have taught you publicly, and from house to house, Testifying both to the Jews, and also to the Greeks, repentance toward God, and faith toward our Lord Jesus Christ. And now, behold, I go bound in the spirit unto Jerusalem, not knowing the things that shall befall me there: Save that the Holy Ghost witnesseth in every city, saying that bonds and afflictions abide me. But none of these things move me, neither count I my life dear unto myself, so that I might finish my course with joy, and the ministry, which I have received of the Lord Jesus, to testify the gospel of the grace of God. And now, behold, I know that ye all, among whom I have gone preaching the kingdom of God, shall see my face no more." Acts 20:19-25. "NONE OF THESE THINGS MOVE ME" floated out of those verses as Reba Jean read them aloud and swirled through the very air of the Library.

Reba Jean searched some more through the Ancient One and soon found the other verses that had so emblazoned themselves upon her heart in recent weeks. *"But thanks be to God, which giveth us the victory through our Lord Jesus Christ. Therefore, my beloved brethren, be ye stedfast, unmoveable, always abounding in the work of the Lord, forasmuch as ye know that your labour is not in vain in the Lord."* 1 Corinthians 15:57-58.

She almost sobbed as she tried to get Lady Jane to realize that all their trauma, all the pain, and all the memories were not to move them or hinder them from serving King Abba. They could influence her, but only in the ways that she allowed them to. She gulped as the rush of thoughts and words seemed to tumble all out of her. Reba Jean rubbed her face with her hands and felt a slight headache lingering; she so wanted Lady Jane to understand what she had learned. Finally, she grabbed Lady Jane's hand, bowed her head, and just let her thoughts course through their hands in a telepathic connection.

Lady Jane jerked at the onslaught of thoughts, but they were invigorating, not tormenting. Reba Jean had received comfort and help from the Overseer in the last few weeks and wanted Lady Jane to absorb it all, as well. Once the thoughts had been absorbed by the two women, they both collapsed on the floor, rubbing their faces as if to smooth out their features. Stretching, pulling back their hair in synchronous motions, they seemed to mirror each other, as well they should—they were just parts of the whole.

Reba Jean felt her headache try to intensify, and her stomach rumbled either in protest of her mental exercise or just trying to distract her. She wanted to spend this day writing and did not want to be distracted by her bodily dysfunctions or anything else. She moved away from Lady Jane to find her writing desk that, once again, was plastered with notes from the thoughts that she needed to capture and write down. That task of organizing those notes seemed daunting; she needed to be more organized instead of just scribbling things down and having to sort through them later.

It was time to start a new chapter in her book. She might not be as far along as she thought, but this book was being written based upon what God showed her, not her own deadlines. She was a bit surprised that she had not poured out her angst upon the pages after all that she had gone through in the last couple of weeks. Then, she realized that it was probably better to focus on how not to be moved by trauma and to find victory instead of being a victim.

"None of these things move me…" mumbled Reba Jean as she began a new chapter in her book about influences.

Chapter 9

Reba Jean looked at the chapter number and realized that this number signified fruit, specifically fruit of the Spirit! The previous chapter should have been about "new beginnings," and in a way, she thought it had been. She felt a few shattered shards in her heart heal as she realized that she had a new perspective, and this would bear spiritual fruit in her life and Library. Fidgeting with the stuff on her desk, she finished the cold remnant of her morning coffee, organized her scraps of notes, and felt almost reluctant to write about treasures for the heart. She had been so looking forward to this since her last entry a week ago. Her desk was ready, she had the time, she had the titles, but she did not seem to have the words burning in her to be put down on paper.

She did not want to write something that the Lord did not give her. Swiping the side of her face with her hand, she felt at a loss. She almost felt like crying; she finally had the time and opportunity to write, and it was as if she had writer's block. Reba Jean looked at her notes and her titles and decided that she would just organize the thoughts and see where they led, if at all. Maybe God wanted her to wait on Him as He had before. She rubbed her neck almost in irritation; patience and waiting were a fruit that was not growing very well in her life. She grimaced, knowing that this was probably the exact lesson that she was supposed to get from this seeming exercise in futility. It was almost lunchtime; she literally had the entire rest of the day. Her husband knew she wanted to write all day, and he was minding the recalcitrant puppy. "OK," Reba Jean mumbled to herself, "go through these notes, assign them to titles, and see where it leads, step by step."

Reba Jean went down to the kitchen table, spread open her notes and Bible, and began to organize all the thoughts and verses on treasure that God had given her in the last weeks. Then she took a break, checked on the dogs and the hummingbird feeders, soaked in some of the heated stillness of the outdoors, and picked tomatoes. She gave a disgusted look at the bad spots on them, how applicable to the chapter she was writing. Her vines had born fruit, but some were unripe, some cankered, so just plain rotten and not useful. She saved what she could and sliced one into some sandwiches for her husband's lunch. Her life seemed to mirror the type of fruit she had just picked. Frowning, she wondered how she could change her plants both spiritually and agriculturally.

Glancing at the devotional titles that she had just gathered thoughts for, she had a feeling those were the key, spiritually. If she was able to write all of these, she would be over the halfway mark in her devotional. This chapter in the novel could be the halfway chapter, even if the pages were not enough yet to count as halfway. Pondering the significance of the halfway mark, she knew she had learned a lot, but the next half would be a testament to how much she would put it into practice and bear good fruit.

Still feeling a reluctance to actually start writing in the devotional, she decided to wander off and distract herself. She was not entirely sure if there was a check in her spirit or if she was putting up her own stumbling blocks. She wanted to catch up on all these entries, but it did feel like a closing of a time period in her life when she did. However, she knew God would probably not give her any more until she had completed these first. Was it fear of failure that was holding her back? She found that she assumed she was failing God all the time, and that was not born of faith but fear. Did she need more prayer before she started? That wouldn't hurt, but she just felt a pause, a hmm, it was hard to describe it, almost a restless stillness. That sounded like an oxymoron, but that's how it felt—a quiet, unsettled feeling.

Reba Jean saved her manuscript and went to take a break from writing. She still had the rest of the day, hopefully, to work on the devotional; she just wanted to be in the right mindset, or was it heartset? After some reluctance, Reba Jean made herself truly organize her notes; soon, the words seemed to fall into place, and she began typing in earnest. Hours later, with a few breaks in between, she crossed that halfway milestone in her devotional and even added an additional entry.

During one of her short breaks, she spoke aloud in the "echoey" chambers of her mind that she wished the Lady Constance or Lady Diane were around to inspire her. She fed off of them and the way God used them to speak to her. Moments later, she received a message from the Lady Constance! Oh, how good God was to her. It was exactly what she needed; she even got permission to quote Lady Constance.

While looking through her notes, Reba Jean found a verse that she knew she wanted to use in her book. *"Cast thy burden upon the LORD, and he shall sustain thee: he shall never suffer the righteous to be moved."* Psalms 55:22. Another verse reference in her notes caught her eye, and she looked that one up as well. Of course, she couldn't just stop at one verse, so she read the verses around it. *"I have set the LORD always before me: because he is at my right hand, I shall not be moved. Therefore my heart is glad, and my glory rejoiceth: my flesh also shall rest in hope. For thou wilt not leave my soul in hell; neither wilt thou suffer thine Holy One to see corruption. Thou wilt shew me the path of life: in thy presence is fulness of joy; at thy right hand there are pleasures for evermore."* Psalms 16:8-11. There was the UN-movable theme again.

Reba Jean knew she needed to be steadfast, immovable, not swayed by the influences of the flesh. It really was important who she hung around; regardless of how much you might think you are strong, you'll only be as strong as the people you surround yourself with. Paging through some of the other Scripture she had found, she landed in Proverbs. *"He that walketh with wise men shall be wise: but a companion of fools shall be destroyed. Evil pursueth sinners: but to the righteous good shall be repayed. A good man leaveth an inheritance to his children's children: and the wealth of the sinner is laid up for the just."* Proverbs 13:20-22. Well, that certainly summed it up correctly.

Reba Jean looked again at the message from Lady Constance, and the verse "by their fruits you shall know them" came to mind. Lady Constance stated that her "fruit absolutely MUST show for others to KNOW that I am a Christian. I don't need to take a day off of bearing fruit for the Lord. Even though I am continuing to grow... that fruit has to SHINE for Him!"

Reba Jean pondered shiny fruit and remembered how often we polish an apple, even stores polish or wax fruit to make it look more appealing. She stated this thought to Lady Constance, who replied, "If we are dull fruit...no one is gonna believe we are Christians. If we are rotten...we just get thrown out, tossed to the side, fed to the animals. But if our fruit shines...people are going to want to know WHO we are SHINING for!"

Together, they discussed her books and how the Lord was using her life to affect, in other words, to influence others. Lady Constance reminded her, "We grow through pain; it tests our faith. It strengthens our walk. If we don't go through the pain, then how can we ever see God's Hand in our lives through those painful times? How would we KNOW we can trust Him and that he is right there through it all?" Growth can be painful, but it does influence us, and the fruit we bear will influence others. Reba Jean did not want to be a bitter crab apple but a shiny, juicy, delicious fruit that others would want to have what she had- The Lord Jesus!

She reached a stopping point in her writing; she was caught up on everything, and it felt good. It was time to start supper. She was ready for the next onslaught of devotional entries that she was sure the Lord would send her way as treasure for her heart. This chapter on fruit-bearing had taken such a lovely turn, and she sent a "thank You" to her Heavenly Father for giving her just what she needed. These milestones were vivid markers on her journey to wherever God was taking her. She had learned so much; now, she just needed to apply it daily!

A few days later, she sat down again to write some more. Why she often felt that the Lord would stop sending her material for her devotional entries was silly. Every time she finished whatever He had given her, He sent her more, sometimes individually, others in batches. She was excited about this, and it thrilled her when God showed her something to treasure in her heart and share with others. She mentally ran through the various aspects of the recent days and sat back with a satisfied sense of productive accomplishment. She had started to use the blue butterfly notebook that Lady Constance had given her to put all of her notes in. It wasn't neat, and that bothered her OCD a bit, but it was better than scraps of paper all over the place.

She thought about her OCD. She worked hard not to let it be a real issue in her life. The recent interaction with her father showed her that much of what she thought she got from her mother might also be from him too. She realized that her defeatist attitude might have been a learned behavior. Her husband told her that once she recognized it, it would be easier to deal with. A verse in James came to mind, and she opened up that book to see what it said. The verses around it were all pertinent as well.

"Do not err, my beloved brethren. Every good gift and every perfect gift is from above, and cometh down from the Father of lights, with whom is no variableness, neither shadow of turning. Of his own will begat he us with the word of truth, that we should be a kind of firstfruits of his creatures. Wherefore, my beloved brethren, let every man be swift to hear, slow to speak, slow to wrath: For the wrath of man worketh not the righteousness of God. Wherefore lay apart all filthiness and

91

superfluity of naughtiness, and receive with meekness the engrafted word, which is able to save your souls. But be ye doers of the word, and not hearers only, deceiving your own selves. For if any be a hearer of the word, and not a doer, he is like unto a man beholding his natural face in a glass: For he beholdeth himself, and goeth his way, and straightway forgetteth what manner of man he was. But whoso looketh into the perfect law of liberty, and continueth therein, he being not a forgetful hearer, but a doer of the work, this man shall be blessed in his deed. If any man among you seem to be religious, and bridleth not his tongue, but deceiveth his own heart, this man's religion is vain. Pure religion and undefiled before God and the Father is this, To visit the fatherless and widows in their affliction, and to keep himself unspotted from the world." James 1:16-27.

She pondered that familiar passage and knew the truth of it. She had just written in her devotional book about the jeweler's illuminated loupe and being a gold digger. She could unlearn wrong behaviors; she could control selfish tendencies. Looking at her notes, she noticed a passage in Colossians had been written down. She did not recall why until she looked that up as well.

"And you, that were sometime alienated and enemies in your mind by wicked works, yet now hath he reconciled In the body of his flesh through death, to present you holy and unblameable and unreproveable in his sight: If ye continue in the faith grounded and settled, and be not moved away from the hope of the gospel, which ye have heard, and which was preached to every creature which is under heaven; whereof I Paul am made a minister;" Colossians 1:21-23. She had been alienated and enemies in her mind by wicked works, but if she continued in the faith grounded and settled—there was that thought again, unmovable!

With the refrain "none of these things move me" ringing through her mind, she listened with half an ear to her husband's questions, replying accordingly. It had been a good week. She really hoped the women's conference on Saturday would be the perfect way to finish strong. Lately, she had gone to meetings and services at church, fully expecting God to speak to her, to even give her something to write about. Sure enough, He always did. She had even written up a long outline about "So much the more" and given it to her associate pastor to use if so inspired. He had teased her that he would preach better if she wrote better. She had retorted in kind, but that little niggle of doubt had tried to creep in. He hadn't even read the outline, so she knew it wasn't based on that. He had already used one of her lessons on the radio and another in Sunday school, so obviously, he was joking.

Reba Jean figured she was about finished writing for the day unless God gave her something more. She felt like she was in a good place; maybe she would check on Lady Constance to see what she thought about the devotional they were studying together. It stated some fruit of the Spirit as attitudes, and that really seemed too shallow of a definition or explanation for Reba Jean. She was no expert on Scripture or on writing about it, but sometimes she was tired of oversimplification and "fluff." She was a gold digger and wanted to really find the treasure that was to be unearthed in Scripture.

The puppy whined to go outside, and she enjoyed the storm rolling in as she listened to the puppy bark at something unseen in the nighttime environment. They had named the puppy Paprika, Peppy for short. The big dog they named Lesa. After coming inside, her husband gave her a piece of pie. She connected with her sister and shared some conversation with her. She had completely forgotten to check on Lady Constance. She had, however, sent an excited text to her editor about the three devotional entries that she had written that day.

Closing her eyes as she relished the sweet treat that the pie gave her, she let her mind run through the Library for a few minutes. She did not even think how this would affect the Library itself, but she would soon hear about it from Lady Jane.

Lady Jane had been enjoying her week; she had not heard from her mistress, and except for some odd, dark tendrils that tried to attack her out of nowhere, she felt as free as the blue butterfly that drifted on the breeze. Those pesky tendrils would need to be sorted, but she wasn't going to think them back into action. She twirled around and watched her skirt float out around her like a lacy parasol. She stumbled a bit, got her feet tangled, and landed on the floor with a giggle and an unladylike snort. She sat there for a minute, just basking in the peace that felt so healing and sublime. With her eyes closed, she thought she heard the sound of footsteps walking through the Library. She sniffed the air—nothing. She slowly opened her eyes, fully expecting to see Reba Jean or something—nothing, no one…

Lady Jane looked around fearfully. Had some rapscallion found its way into the Library? She still heard the footsteps, but there was nothing attached to them. Curiosity and fear coursed through her, so she spun her head around, looking for the nearest artifact that would help her. Her eyes landed on the Oil Lamp shining comfortingly from its usual place. She jumped up, grabbed it, and shone its blazing light around. It illuminated the footprints that were being made, and she decided to follow these prints to see where they went. Maybe she could figure out who or what was making these footprints without being seen.

She tracked the steps to the corridor of hope, found them in the prayer closet, and retraced them back and forth between these areas quite a few times. They led to the Ancient One and to the writing desk, and then they went back to the prayer closet. She noticed impressions on the floor that were deeper than the footprints. Leaning down, she put her hand on those deeper prints and felt sadness and then thankfulness tingle through her whole being. With a sigh of relief, she knew that her mistress had somehow made all of these tracks without actually being in the Library.

Closing her eyes, she tried to mentally connect with her mistress, wherever she might be. She hoped she wasn't alienated in her own mind, as she had been on other occasions. She waited expectantly and tried not to doubt or be impatient. Licking her lips, she tasted chocolate pudding. Uhm, this was not the connection she had in mind. Giggling and savoring the sweetness, she tried again to connect with Reba Jean telepathically. You would think that since they were basically the same person, this would have been instantaneous; however, Reba Jean was not your usual middle-aged woman.

Reba Jean rubbed her nose; something was making it tingly. Was it all the cats? She felt an ache settle on her shoulders like a weight. She scratched an itch on her arm and wondered why she was all twitchy after such a good night, in fact, a very good week. She felt like she was forgetting something, but it was hard to figure out what that could be if she couldn't remember. She was getting really fidgety and twitchy now; everything started itching. There were no venomous vines, no itchy cats, no Conté; she rubbed her neck and felt like she needed to get out of the room.

Peppy jumped on her leg and whined yet again, and Reba Jean pelted for the staircase to the Library. Her empty bowl of pudding pie was left twirling on her desk. Peppy disappeared to its master's arms, and Reba Jean slammed the Library door shut. Ahhh, the peace of the Library, she almost snorted. This place was so rarely peaceful; she had better be careful what she thought about.

Wandering around, she noticed the Oil Lamp was not in its usual place, and the first prickle of fear raised the hair on her arms. Looking around, she tried to see if she could see the light from the Lamp so that it could light her path. It was nighttime, so there was no sun shining through the azure windows to illuminate the cavernous expanse of the Library. Soon, she saw a dim glow, and she headed in that direction. It seemed to take forever to finally turn the corner and see Lady Jane holding forth the shining Lamp towards her.

The two halves of the whole looked at each other; both had questions all over their faces. The misty tendrils even formed themselves into question marks all around them. Reba Jean brushed her bangs off her forehead and shrugged. Quietly, they both sat down right where they had met each other, and the Oil Lamp was placed in the middle between them. The lovely glow seemed to calm them both, and soon, a lovely conversation ensued. Reba Jean shared her week, the answer to prayer about the fear of the DMV, how the lovely ladies there had seemed almost like angels, and how she had been able to sow a seed about prayer to one of them. Then, with an ache in her heart, she prayed for one of her co-workers, whose name was Angel. Angel might not be saved, but Reba Jean had been trying to be a living witness to her. This week, it was determined that Angel had probably lost her unborn child. Reba Jean had gone repeatedly to the prayer closet about Angel and her situation. Lady Jane listened as she talked about hope anew over the re-connection with the daughter-in-law. Together, they prayed for the niece who had asked for prayer about a situation she was facing. Reba Jean also prayed for the women's conference, that it would be full of God's Word and help for her and the other women. She did not want fluff and all nonsense; she wanted to get something from the Lord—not the door prizes.

There was a pause in conversation, and they could hear the pages of the Ancient One turning on its marble pedestal. Together, they rose to read what it was beckoning them to see. Psalm 37 was open, and verse upon verse seemed to just speak to everything they had shared with each other. What a perfect way to end the night—in the Word of King Abba.

As they were about to go their separate ways, the mystery of the mental footsteps had been solved, albeit the concept was a bit unnerving to Lady Jane. She remembered again the dark, smoky tendrils that had attacked her. Lady Jane almost mentioned them to Reba Jean but decided not to ruin the peace, as she was sure that it would. She made a mental note—ha, well, that sounded like an oxymoron—but she knew she would need to mention it to her mistress. Maybe she would the next time it happened or the next time they were together.

Lady Jane used the Lamp to help Reba Jean find the door back to the living room, and then she settled it back in its assigned spot. Its comforting glow seemed to wrap Lady Jane in a hug, almost like a warm blanket, and she decided that she was going to stay by the Lamp tonight. She did not think the dark tendrils would attack her in the light of the Lamp.

Chapter 10

Reba Jean made it through a very busy week—barely. She really did not think she was going to survive, but God brought along Lady Diane again in the most timely manner. Their conversation was exactly what Reba Jean needed. She saw the obvious reasons that God wanted her to keep this job. The words "unmovable" and "opportunity" were not obscure in their meanings. Lady Constance lamented to her that they did not spend time in God's Word as much together. This sparked a long time of meditation for Reba Jean that very day. She was excited to share with Lady Constance the thoughts that the Lord had given her. Their study of Mary and Martha was convicting, and Reba Jean found that her other devotionals and Scripture studies seemed to go right along with each other. She knew this was done purposefully by her Lord and Savior.

Reba Jean stared off into space for a few minutes. She had sat down to write in *Treasure for the Heart*, and it had turned into three individual entries based on a recurring theme of wisdom. Pondering if that was the next treasure that she was to be collecting, she wondered if she had even collected the others. With that thought in mind, she decided to go visit Lady Jane in the Library.

The steps were taken at a meandering pace, almost like she was in a daydream. Lazily, opening the large ornate doors, she felt the smooth grain of the wood beneath her hands as they swung inwardly. She stopped a minute; these doors seemed to move differently at different times, and that puzzled her. Shrugging her shoulders at the unsolved mystery, she let them swoosh behind her and inhaled the air in the Library. She puzzled over the fact that sometimes the entrance to the Library was a single door and other times it was a large archway with heavy double doors. This surely had some sort of meaning, but the solution to the mystery was as misty as the tendrils and golden dust motes that floated down from the ether.

Catching a few golden dust motes in her throat, she coughed and then giggled. Just ahead in the atrium, Reba Jean spotted Lady Jane off to one side. She was sitting on the table next to the Oil Lamp. This table blocked the entrance to the Crimson Vault. The babbling of the Fountain, the glow of the Lamp, the golden dust motes, and the wispy tendrils of thoughts all made the place feel welcoming and peaceful. Reba Jean, however, could hear Sir Theo fussing at Peppy, who had tried to follow her into the Library.

He knew she needed time to write, think, rest, and regroup, and Peppy was very distracting for this process. Sir Theo had been very perceptive lately and put in much effort to help her survive her busy weeks. His suggestions may not always work for her, but he was trying to help. She sent a telepathic hug to him in his office as she went to inquire of Lady Jane about her current position.

Lady Jane saw her mistress coming towards her and saw that perplexed look on her face. How could she explain that she was hearing ominous footsteps that didn't sound like Reba Jean walking through or that she felt like voices were coming from the well again? She felt fear prickle on the back of her neck just at the thought of it. These odd happenings felt foreboding, not comforting.

Reba Jean sat down on the table next to her avatar companion and just looked at her. She seemed to want to stay around the Oil Lamp that symbolized the Light and the Spirit. This was not a bad thing, but why was the Light and Spirit not permeating the entire Library? She looked around and saw strongboxes, stacks of treasures, faith, patience, love, hope, prayer, praise, and many others. Thankfully, the treasures were still there, yet somehow, they did not feel like they were enough of a comfort to Lady Jane to give her the strength to leave the table.

Reba Jean did not say anything; she just put her arm around her avatar and sat with her. Maybe the silence would give an answer to the unasked questions. Reba Jean listened to see if she could figure out why Lady Jane did not seem to want to get off the table. The electronic sounds from Sir Theo's Library did not seem threatening; if anything, they sounded victorious. The praise room was humming something, but it was light and indistinct. Was that the problem? Should the volume be checked, or should the praises be increased? The pages of the Ancient One were not flipping, but this did not alarm her. Off in the distance, she felt hope send out rays of comfort from that side of the Library.

Waiting seemed to be the only way to resolve this; nothing seemed out of the ordinary to Reba Jean. She began to daydream as she sat next to Lady Jane and soon forgot that she was supposed to be listening. The table, however, was not meant to be a chair, and it wasn't long before she wanted to get down. She slanted her eyes at Lady Jane, but the lady of the Library was not going to budge. Reba Jean shrugged her shoulders and began to walk through the Library.

Heading towards the aisles in the back, the misty tendrils got heavier and darker and seemed to prick her as she walked through them. Swatting at them, she chose not to let them reveal themselves and their intent. She just kept pushing through them to see where she would end up. She felt like she was going around in circles and getting twisted up in prickly tendrils; however, this made her feel like calling for the Golden Sword. She inhaled, straightened her shoulders as if she was about to do battle, and pushed her way onward to, well, to wherever.

Hearing the sound of water, she found herself at the Whispering Well. Sitting down on the edge, she smacked away the dark tendrils that kept trying to attack her. Her eyes enlarged with an idea, and she reached her hands into the well, scooped up the Living Water, and rubbed her neck, arms, and exposed areas. The dark tendrils shrank back in horror at the barrier of Living Water now on their target. She sat on the edge of the well and almost wished she could hear the voices, just to see what they were saying. The Living Water served as protection and a filter. Maybe it would be possible to hear voices that would be a good influence on her.

She closed her eyes in concentration and listened; the dark tendrils couldn't distract her now. It was fairly quiet, to begin with, then she thought she heard Lady Constance, RaeAnne, and Lady Diane, the echoes of conversations they had had. Her eyes still closed, she listened and soon she heard Amy Lynne, a sister who had asked for marital advice. Then she heard Angel, and she immediately began praying for this sad soul who so desperately needed Lord Rabboni and the Comforter.

As the weeks went by, Reba Jean struggled with so many issues. She found it increasingly difficult to go to work. It was a daily battle; she longed to be home again to write and handle ministry opportunities, along with taking care of the house and zoo. She knew it was ironic because, just a few months prior, she was complaining about the zoo and how it was stressing her out. Her weekly conversations with Lady Diane were sometimes challenging and, at other times, aggravating. She often felt that Lady Diane wanted to "fix her." She had received great results in her own life from counseling and other avenues the Lord had led her to help her deal with her trauma. Reba Jean knew that counseling was a good tool, even Lady Dana had offered that to her. However, other voices of influence were louder and may be more influential because they told her what she wanted to hear.

She did not want to go to counseling; she just wanted to have some solitude and let her writing be therapy along with the in-depth Scripture study that she was doing. She knew she had some bad attitudes that needed to be dealt with, and yet it seemed that family often triggered those bad attitudes. As much as she had thought she was dealing with her reactions and her thoughts, she refused to go back to the Library for months. She did not want to clean up any messes, fight any minions, console Lady Jane, or dust off any treasures. There was just too much going on in her physical realm that she had no desire to deal with the mental realm. The thought of dark tendrils soon got lost in the shuffle, and Lady Jane just seemed to be an imaginary playmate of yesteryear.

The concept of influence was never far from her mind every day. She had spent some time with Daisy May and Skye and knew that they were watching her closely on a regular basis. Lady Constance might expect her to be "more spiritual," but she at least understood that Reba Jean was still working through issues. She did not mind when Reba Jean was raw and open with her as they studied together.

Even though work was a constant battle, the Lord kept showing her exactly why He said it was an opportunity to witness. He was very clear that she was not to move from where He had placed her until He said it was time. Her continued conversations with Angel finally led her to believe that Angel was possibly saved; she listened to the Bible on audio, and she was going back to church. She believed in the power of prayer. Reba Jean had the unexpected joy of hearing that other co-workers had clear testimonies of salvation. As doors around her seemed to open and close for opportunities to shine the light of the glorious gospel, it was the unexpected surprise of being asked to pray for someone or finding a like-minded believer, all while wearing the same company uniform, that made it worthwhile. This did not stop her from longing to be back home again, immersed in her writing, but it sure did make it obvious why she was not yet allowed to have that desire.

Reba Jean was still writing the devotional about *Treasure for the Heart*, but her novel was untouched. She felt it was important to concentrate and focus on what the Lord wanted her to share about things that pertained to spiritual value. One might think this was like having a double mind; she was not really taking care of the Library or its treasure collection, yet she was absorbed in writing about spiritual treasures. As time went by, she became acutely aware of this and how her relationship with her husband was just as unsteady. Their communication issues were often the catalyst of the outbursts. That man sure did know how to trigger her moods and reactions, and not in a pleasing manner. Patience was not a treasure she was collecting much of these days.

However, she was beginning to see the difference in her understanding of things from listening and focusing on spiritual matters. For instance, all this time she had been considering the concept of influence and its effect on her and others. It wasn't until she saw a comment by the emissary of Stone's Corner that she opened her mind to something a bit more profound. He was thanking other emissaries for the "Impact" they had on his life. An impact was much deeper and left more marks, nay, even indentations, than any surface influences. All this time, she had just looked at the surface tension, the shallow wafting of voices and thoughts, and had not paid attention to what was making deeper impressions upon her heart and mind.

Reba Jean knew she would need to deal with the Library, her communication issues with her husband, along with making herself keep working until God allowed her to stop. These were not just influences, for they were leaving a mark on her life. She needed them to leave the right impact, not more scars that needed counseling or therapy or medication. These remedies were not bad, but she just did not want to have to need them if there was a way to deal with these issues instead of storing them.

She knew she needed to go to the Library soon. She wanted to visit the corridor of hope. So much had happened since the last sorrow-filled visit. She could paint the walls with joy, and she knew that she needed to resolve the tendrils of dark, evil thoughts and check for cracks and rats, but it just seemed like way too much work. Surely, Lady Jane would be fine as long as she stayed by the celestial artifacts. Wouldn't she?

Chapter 11

Lady Jane had not seen her mistress in months; oh, she could hear her walking around at times. However, her actual presence was nowhere to be found. The Library went through its usual cycling of horror, peace, and sporadic surprises. Lady Jane never knew what each day would bring; it seemed that every day was full of each category, and she was getting used to it. Bright, golden radiance would be blotted out by dark tendrils, to then be whisked away by a fresh breeze from the celestial realm. The corridor of hope was ablaze with sounds of cries and cooing from the little miracle that was once again back in their lives.

The treasures were still in stacks; some seemed to glow and grow, while others seemed to collect dust or get slid back into the dark recesses of the cavernous aisles. Lady Jane did not like to go to the Whispering Well or even walk down the aisles of books as a librarian should do regularly. It was too dangerous, for you never knew if some book would open and its contents run rampant throughout. Lady Jane was suspicious of every noise, and she had a feeling that somehow General Nefarious or Captain Insidious had been able to maneuver their minions back into the Library through otherwise unknown means. She could almost hear the buzzing of murder hornets and feel the choking, itchy hold of the poisonous vines that had invaded not long ago. She shivered and scratched the scars from the vines and the rat bites. She knew that the Ancient One said that it did not give the spirit of fear but of power and of love and of a sound mind. Someone needed to remind Reba Jean of that!

Lady Jane spent her time around the Oil Lamp or the Fountain of Living Waters just to be safe. She did not go to her boudoir and only took brief visits to the portico of peace. She found it safer to stay away from Sir Theo's office; he seemed so volatile. Whether it was his health or mental issues, she was not sure, but she knew Reba Jean was having daily struggles with him.

She sighed; she did not know if she missed her mistress or not. It just seemed like they had parted ways, each to deal with their own living situations. You would not even think that they were really parts of the same whole. She licked her dry lips, heard Peppy whining at the door of the Library, and almost felt like she was in a prison of her own making. She could open the door, couldn't she? Lady Jane did not ever venture outside the Library; even the portico was an attached room to the Library. She had never been to the living room or the actual prayer closet that the one up here duplicated. That prayer closet had turned into a storage room in the Library. It had baby stuff in it and boxes and totes of all sorts of keepsakes. It looked nothing like a prayer closet, more like, well, more like a closet that needed cleaning. She had a feeling that it was the same as Reba Jean's prayer closet downstairs—a mess of clutter and no place to pray, only a place to be distracted and disgusted.

As her stomach growled, Lady Jane wondered what there was to eat. She only had real food if someone brought it to her. Most of the time, her food was "food for thought," spiritual food, or imaginary tea parties. What was she hungry enough to eat? She had a steady diet lately of bad thoughts, bitter fruit, bruised feelings, and nibbles of sweet blessings.

Honestly, she just longed for a long, cool drink of Living Water and maybe a hug from the celestial realm. She glanced around and saw Goodness and Mercy staying reassuringly close. A golden vial appeared with the word JOY engraved upon its iridescent side. She looked inside; it was nearly empty. Askance, she grabbed it close and ran to the Ancient One. Flipping precious pages, she found the passage she was looking for: *"Hitherto have ye asked nothing in my name: ask, and ye shall receive, that your joy may be full."* John 16:24

"Oh, Lord Rabboni, my joy is nearly empty. Will You please fill me with your joy?" breathed Lady Jane in prayer. She watched as the pages flipped to another passage in response. *"Now the God of hope fill you with all joy and peace in believing, that ye may abound in hope, through the power of the Holy Ghost. And I myself also am persuaded of you, my brethren, that ye also are full of goodness, filled with all knowledge..."* Romans 15:13-14.

Lady Jane was hungry for spiritual food, and here she could have her fill of joy, goodness, hope, and knowledge, only found in the Ancient One, the Word of God, from her King Abba. Leaning her face downward, she touched the Ancient One with her cheek and felt as if she was caressed in return. Peace that passed all understanding seemed to wrap around her like a safe blanket. She could rest secure in this peace, even when the Library was in a chaotic cycle, and her mistress was nowhere to be found.

Downstairs away from the Library and its avatar, Reba Jean felt the roller-coaster effects of her life. She dressed for a birthday party for her granddaughter, selecting articles of clothing that were given to her by the matriarchs in her family. She chose butterfly socks and managed to enjoy herself in spite of her husband's roller-coaster moods.

Her face had really broken out into sores that would not heal. She had cleansed them and cared for them but always managed to pick at them. She thought about the word "roller coaster" as she wiped blood off her cheek. The dermatologist scoffed at the thought of her phone giving her the sores. In fact, he was not even concerned about it; he treated the blue nevus on her arm and told her to come back in a year.

Reba Jean worked hard to catch up on housework, write her devotional entries, and try not to be cranky, as she never knew what her husband was going to say or do next. Oh, she was aware of possible combination causes of his outbursts, but she was not really able to fix them. She just rode the roller coaster, trying not to be sick of him or from him. Rubbing her infected cheek, she wondered again if the sores were from stress, much like her chewed fingernails that were bleeding again.

Her husband was heading to bed, and she knew she needed to get there as well. She had too full of a schedule, and it was not going to get any better if she got too tired to handle it all. Reba Jean needed to tend her face and study over the problem she had of needing a prayer closet that didn't look and feel like a cluttered storage room. She knew she could handle all these crazy ups and downs and gut-wrenching turns in life if she had a consistent place to pray. It had been such an ongoing issue for years. She would finally get some victory and feel like she was praying as she ought, only to lose momentum or peace in that space.

Reba Jean prayed often, but not in a prayer closet, and she longed for that. With a sigh, she went to wash her face and pray about a place to pray that was all hers—hers and the Lord's. After a few more days of agonizing frustration, she realized that there was no other place than her current prayer closet.

With grim determination, Reba Jean strode into the room that had once again become cluttered and messy and worked long and hard to clean it up. Once this was finally accomplished, she expected it to feel, well, holy. Except it didn't. It wasn't the room that was meant to be holy; it was HER!

As time passed, it was still a struggle to have the willpower to go to her prayer closet. Some days, it was easy, but often, it was a session in near futility. As the holidays neared, the room became cluttered yet again. Reba Jean, however, was more than determined to keep it as her prayer closet. She patiently waited for the holidays to be over, cleaned and organized it yet again. This time, she had more success, and soon, she felt like she was learning and growing again.

Her face healed, she started growing her nails, she remonstrated her husband for his angry outbursts, and she sought the Lord for strength to do His will. After a couple of months of consistently begging God for His Strength to do His will, He reminded her through Scripture that she already had His Strength! She then asked why she couldn't feel it. The answer was not long in coming. The JOY of the Lord was her strength; she needed to stop whining, be thankful, and SING! Sing?! She did not sing; she croaked, warbled, hit every wrong note, couldn't carry a tune, but sing, no, that was not the word for the sounds that came forth from her larynx. However, the answer was obvious: she was not going to feel the strength until she had so much joy that she would burst forth in songs of praise.

Chapter 12

Lady Jane was still curious about going outside the Library. After ruminating about it for a time, she realized that she would not be able to actually go OUT. She could go to the Living Room or the Prayer Closet, but she would not be able to actually go out into the Terrestrial Realm. However, she could look out the cerulean blue windows up there to see that realm. She looked around trying to figure out how to safely climb up to the windows and look out. Closing her eyes, she cast about for any solutions. Then she laughed; she was in the Library. The Library could do nearly anything she imagined!

With a giggle, she grabbed some misty tendrils and yanked on them; with an artistic flare, she fashioned them into what appeared to be a spiral staircase that looked like it was made of wrought iron. However, she made sure it was on wheels; this way, it could be moved to wherever she wanted it to within the Library. She may not want to always look out the window or see what was going on outside the Library.

With a shove and a sigh, Lady Jane maneuvered the rolling staircase to the windows high above the atrium. Her steps had a spring to them as she bounded up the staircase, expecting, well, who knew what to expect. She peered out the windows and felt an uneasy feeling in the pit of her stomach. She could see everything that Reba Jean could see, and now she realized how protected she was within the confines of the Library.

Lady Jane descended the newly formed staircase, a bit wiser. As she stood in the atrium, she heard Reba Jean mentally walking through the Library again. The dust motes often showed her footprints on the floor to trace where she went in the Library. Lady Jane followed the footprints and entered a sitting room. It was surrounded by bookshelves that seemed to contain special books. These were separate from the aisles upon aisles of books in the main Library.

Twirling around at a rustling of pages, Lady Jane found a book that had opened on a small, secretary-style desk, with the roll top lid and cubicles, as well as little drawers with golden handles. Fascinated by the little desk and the open book, Lady Jane sat down and began reading. Oh! This was book three. It wasn't the manuscript from downstairs; no, it was all the plots and scenarios that Reba Jean thought about during the day that never seemed to actually make it onto paper.

Another book lay next to it; this was the devotional that Lord Rabboni was helping her write. She saw another book off to the side of the desk. She opened it and saw thoughts and ideas for a fourth book in the series. Lady Jane glanced around and found a cute, comfortable chair to settle into. She began to read plots and scenarios that may never make it to paper, but oh, boy, were they enjoyable to read!

Her eyes got huge when she read how to handle the scary dark tendrils that had plagued her recently or how Captain Insidious might be using those tendrils like puppet strings to influence the Library. She continued reading and soon sprang to her feet. These ideas might not make it into the book, but they could make her life better in the Library! Lady Jane had just read how her mistress wondered if Lady Jane needed to be stronger and become a warrior princess in the Library instead of cowering by the Oil Lamp, always living in fear. Those dark tendrils were the spirit of fear! She was given power and a sound mind, according to the Ancient One; why was she allowing those tendrils of fear to influence and control her?!

She paced around the private Library of Reba Jean and felt herself grow more determined to stop being such a sissy. Whirling, she strode out of the room and straight to the pedestal holding the Ancient One. As surely as she had come to expect, Its pages turned to show her exactly what King Abba had been showing Reba Jean the past two days. The joy of the Lord was her strength!

Lady Jane scratched an itch on the back of her neck and realized that the Library was still and hushed, anticipating her next move. With confidence borne from Scripture, she strode to the music room and decided that even if the music was to be inside of her, it wouldn't hurt for the whole Library to hear it! She went to the control panel, blew off a cloud of dust that had settled over it, and cranked up the volume to a proper pulsation of sound.

The burst of praise that crescendoed throughout the recesses of the Library welled up inside of her as well until she burst forth in song to King Abba and Lord Rabboni. Lady Jane found herself smiling from ear to ear. The Library seemed to just glow, and there wasn't any sign of dark, dastardly tendrils threatening to strangle her.

Stretching her arms up and out, she symbolically embraced the Library. Oh, it was good to feel strong and alive again! Lady Jane was so glad that she had found the right answer to her dilemma, but she was even more thankful that Reba Jean had found the same answer! They would both be strong in the Lord and in the power of His might!

"Sing, woman, sing," shouted Lady Jane into the great expanse of the Library. As the echoes ricocheted off distance aisles and walls, their bouncing sound waves made her giggle with glee. With another happy twirl, Lady Jane danced around the Library, touching book titles, swinging misty tendrils as if they were banners, and blowing kisses to the golden dust motes. She polished the Oil Lamp until it fairly glistened, trailed her fingers through the Fountain, flicked the gossamer runner, twirled the Golden Sword a few times in mock battle moves, and then decided to go conquer her fear of the Whispering Well.

Grasping the Golden Sword in her hand, she fastened the suit of armor onto herself and headed for that Whispering Well that seemed to be a cacophony of voices and suggestions, both good and evil. Even if it had the water of the Word of God in it, some voices still seemed to be able to offer untoward suggestions. She wanted to be armed and protected, well, just in case. She also didn't want any wolves surprising her from the dark recesses of the Library.

Sitting on the rim of the Whispering Well, she listened to see if she could discern any of them. Lady Jane heard Lady Matilda, Lady Diane, and Lady Constance as the primary voices. She peered into the water and saw the faces of Skye and Daisy Mae, and then she saw something intriguing. On a little ledge just out of the reach of the water was a book. Had a book fallen into the well? She fashioned a fishing pole and line with hook out of the ever-present tendrils and fished up the book from the ledge. She opened it with trembling hands. After all she lived in the realm where Captain Insidious and General Nefarious seemed to be able to cause havoc on occasions. She did not want to find one of THEIR books!

As she held the book, the title became clear to her—**Sphere of Influence,** it read. Opening to the first pages, she found names written down and little notations next to each name. KJ, Caemyne, Skye, Daisy Mae, Nellie, Larry, Roger, Angel, RaeAnne, Amy Lynne, Hope, Joe Nathan, Hans, and the list went on, page upon page. She recognized some of these names, of course, but some of them were new and even foreign to her.

She tapped her finger on the page she had opened and pondered what this book was. Glancing down at some of the notations, she felt clarity blow away the question marks in her mind. These were the names of the people that Reba Jean was in direct contact with on a regular basis. She wanted to be a good influence on them. Some of these were people that she was witnessing to! Lady Jane hugged the book close to her for a few minutes. Her mistress was determined not just to be a good influence, but she was praying that the Word of God would have a profound, life-changing impact on these people!

This book, as it lay against Lady Jane's chest, seemed to breathe focus and resolve into Lady Jane. It was time, in the early stages of this new year, to help Reba Jean be a godly influence to those within her sphere. Should she put the book back in the well on the ledge, or should she put it in the private Library? Glancing sideways with a smile, she jerked on a golden tendril, and with an unspoken command, it brought her a book. With great care, she penned a copy of this book and returned the original to the ledge on the inside of the well. Gathering her skirt as she stood upright, Lady Jane let it swoosh around her ankles freely. She took a copy of the book to the private Library and placed it on the little writing desk.

She twirled around again, letting her skirt swish around her as if they were dancing to the music that was still pulsating throughout the Library. A soft scratching sound came to her ears, along with a faint whine. Peppy was desperate to get in; she found it interesting that the door was not allowing the puppy in. With a final sashaying swish of her skirt, she opened the door a crack, just enough to let the puppy in but not enough to see what was outside the Library.

She was the warrior princess of the Library. She did not need to tend to the living room or go out into the Terrestrial Realm; she had her hands full here, especially with the fussy puppy!

Reba Jean had not been able to write in what seemed like weeks. She had run scenarios through her mind on a daily basis, jotting down notes to try to remember to use in her third book or in her devotional. These past weeks had been an intense battle of wills—hers or God's. She had finally surrendered, but that felt more like defeat. With determination, she forced herself to submit to God's will, way, and when without knowing His why. Her journal was full of daily Scripture and notes about this battle. She really had no way to transcribe all this into her book as much as she wanted to.

Sneaking into her office, she sat down to write with hopes that she would make some headway. After a few paragraphs, her writing program crashed. It had not saved her latest attempt to write more. With a huff, she brought her laptop to her computer guru husband to try to fix. After updates and tweaking, he handed her back her laptop so she could attempt once again to rewrite what she had tried to plot out earlier.

Reba Jean sat in her chair, lost in thought. She did not have writer's block, but she seemed thwarted at every turn to write. It was time for bed; who was she kidding? Just when she finally got a chance to write, none of the scenarios that she had constructed in her head for weeks seemed to translate onto paper. If she had not been striving for maturity, she sure would have been tempted to give into a temper tantrum that would have made any toddler jealous. However, throwing her laptop or screaming would not help her write better.

The orange cat butted its head against her arm; the zoo wanted to be put to bed. She glanced at the clock and knew it was time to give up in defeat.

Strange noises emanated from the hallway. Whatever was her husband up to? Oh, he was pulling out stuff to pack!

The orange cat continued to rub its head against her as she watched her husband bring out clothes to the table that had been set up in the kitchen. She knew she needed to write about this newest adventure that was soon to be upon them. She glanced at the orange cat and smiled. She and her hubby were going to take a voyage! Their first venture onto the wild seas in a ship!

Chapter 13

Reba Jean struggled with anxiety about security screenings, safe travels, seasickness, and sundry other nerve-wracking scenarios that MIGHT happen. None of those were the issues that haunted their first sea voyage. No, it was their marriage or relationship squabbles from being in close quarters together. Her husband's penchant for narcissism was prevalent during most of the voyage. Reba Jean was sick to death of his selfish preferences, but she tried to just keep silent and seemingly submissive. However, she was internally seething and stewing!

On their way home, a long, long drive from the port back to the countryside, her brother Joe Nathan called, bidding her to say her earthly goodbyes to their father. He was about to step across to the celestial realm in a few short hours. Sure enough, an hour after they dragged their weary bodies into the house, she saw she had missed a call an hour earlier. She called her brother to hear the news that her father was no longer on this side of eternity.

The next day, after some brief sleep, she drove by herself to meet with her brothers, Joe Nathan and J. D., who had flown in for a family meeting. RaeAnne was kept in the loop but did not want to be physically present for the upcoming arrangements. The siblings discussed plans, and then Amika, Joe Nathan's amazing wife, softly urged him to share what their father had confessed upon his deathbed.

With agony, Reba Jean heard that her assumptions about their mother's mental syndrome were indeed true, but it went deeper than that. The barbaric treatment she endured in her childhood to treat then unknown mental issues was torturous and did NOT help her already fractured mind. Their dad apologized to Joe Nathan for the way he had been treated as a child at her hands. He begged his son to forgive their mother and find a way to love her. He said he would. Reba Jean had to take that apology by proxy and find a way to love her mother, as well.

There was no vindication for being right, but it did bring closure. The lifelong lie and lack of working around the mental issues were still hard to process. In fact, the other extreme of the situation had been implemented instead. That their mother was perfect, and everyone else, especially her husband and children, was stupid and defective, was hard to bear as a valid plan to save their mother's weak grasp on reality. Reba Jean had a suspicion that her mother was just acting out how she had been treated as a child and taking her revenge on everyone else.

Reba Jean drove home from the family meeting, feeling numb and yet determined that she needed to tell her own family and RaeAnne what had been revealed. She had somehow expected a bit more of a reaction from RaeAnne concerning this. However, they had often analyzed it and had already realized the symptoms of the Syndrome years earlier. So, it wasn't necessarily all new, just the details of the torture that their mother had been subjected to in her childhood and the addition of the willful concealment of any acceptance or knowledge that this had even occurred. Their childhood and safety had been sacrificed so that their mother could somehow not believe that she herself had any issues. Reba Jean felt so defective and dejected. Yet, she had to remember that God had been very clear that He had allowed her to be born, He had preserved her life, and He had a purpose for her to serve Him. She knew that was true, but now she wondered if some of her issues that she daily battled with were not necessarily sin issues but synapses askew.

She, however, refused to let biological or spiritual battles have victory over her mind and heart.

Reba Jean called her husband on the way home, driving through pouring rain as if the sky was crying for her. He was not happy with the news, much less how it had been delivered after it had been withheld and denied for three-fourths of a century. As they talked, Sir Theo kept insisting he had been so scared that Reba Jean would turn into the same sort of unstable person. He kept insisting he had worked hard to help her not become like that. She began castigating her husband for being more like her mother than she ever had or would be. In his desire to somehow "help" her, he had instead imitated the same undesired behaviors that he thought she needed to be warned away from.

The next week was long and difficult; Sir Theo kept his distance after the very accurate rebuke that she had thrown at him. She had accepted his apology, but her senses were on overload. It was her designated task to notify certain people, fill out the obituary, and still handle work, ministry, family, and mentoring needs as if she was unswayed by the emotional upheaval she was enduring.

By the end of the week, she was starting to tell everyone that she needed to write and have some time to DE-stress. She spoke with her church counselor, Lady Diane, and Lady Matilda and then took time to sit down and write in her novel that Sunday after lunch. Writing was her therapy. She did not get enough time to do it, and the words burning in her mind to be spilled out upon the page actually made it worse when she was not able to sit down and let them pour out of her.

In the midst of her emotional trauma, she had been able to witness to KJ for hours, but with no rebirth yet. Five young people had been saved over the weekend, and she had been able to actually babysit, yes, babysit her grandbaby. Snuggling that precious picture of hope and grace had helped her so much.

So, where did life go from here? Well, now she had to design and print out the pamphlet for the memorial service, and life seemed to be full of so many things to keep track of. She felt her stomach churn and knew that it was going to be a roller coaster for a while.

Reba Jean stopped writing for a minute and did a brief Scripture search on peace. She knew she needed peace for her mind, heart, body, and spirit. She paused and sat for a few minutes, her fingers hovering over the keyboard. There were a few more things to write in this book and another devotional entry to frame out in *Treasure for the Heart*. However, she let the Scripture verses about peace drift over her like a soft hug from her Divine Comforter.

It was about time to go back to the Library and make sense of the storm that she was sure had assailed it the last few weeks. How do you fortify a Library of the Mind that already has built-in structural defects? A Scripture passage immediately sprang forth in answer to her question. *"Speaking to yourselves in psalms and hymns and spiritual songs, singing and making melody in your heart to the Lord; Giving thanks always for all things unto God and the Father in the name of our Lord Jesus Christ; Submitting yourselves one to another in the fear of God."* Ephesians 5:19-21.

Nearly spent but feeling much better, Reba Jean decided to put off a trip to the Library. It would not be good to go up there until she was sure she was strong enough to help Lady Jane with the minions of chaos. Instead, she opened her butterfly notebook to review the notes for the devotional entry she was hoping to write. The bare bones were there, but she did not feel the Spirit ready to flesh it out into something for the written page yet. She wasn't sure if it was her or if He still had some things to show her about this particular entry. She was a bit dejected, feeling like she was the reason this devotional book had not been finished yet. However, she needed to trust God's timing and teaching.

Her eyes glanced over the notes again, but nothing seemed to gel or coalesce. With reluctance, she closed the notebook and decided to rest before the evening service. She was not ready to write anymore; she had no desire to see what Captain Insidious, General Nefarious, or some demonic minion had conjured up in the Library. She just wanted peace, real peace, and that was what she was going to concentrate on. "Peace, peace, wonderful peace, coming down from the Father above, sweep over me soul…" soothing song lyrics flooded her mind and heart as she saved her writing and felt like she had helped her psyche by letting the words pour out onto the digital, soon-to-be-printed page.

Her peace seemed very short-lived as that very night, white-hot anger filled her with a rage that kept her from sleeping. The cover-up just seemed so unforgivable. Reba Jean wrestled with the whole dramatic retelling of her childhood trauma that kept replaying in her mind. She tried to see how they justified that maybe her mother's damaged brain was not able to handle the idea that she wasn't healed or able to function in the real world.

Reba Jean could even see how her mother was trying so hard to prove that she was able to function and be a capable human, except her very zeal to prove that she was had backfired by her inability to have balanced emotions, realistic goals, and normal thought processes. She just kept trying to prove that there was nothing wrong with her and that she was perfect. If there was a defect, it was in the other person. Reba Jean could see how that had affected her own upbringing. Even now, Reba Jean always felt defensive and had to prove that she wasn't stupid or incapable of dealing with life.

So, although she could see how her mother had progressed to this stage, it did not comfort Reba Jean one iota. The fact that her mother had not been guided and held accountable was reprehensible. She was able to fake being "normal" in social and church settings, but she would have complete uncontrolled anger and emotional outbursts within her family without much interference, for fear it would damage her more. This was almost insurmountable for Reba Jean to understand.

The anger she felt had to be released, but it was hours before she finally surrendered it to God. There did not seem to be any rest for Reba Jean, who struggled to come to terms with all this baggage, her mentoring of a very clingy young Christian who was also all drama, and her desire to be a good witness to her co-worker. It became too much for Reba Jean after a few days, and the message from her Preacher about staying by the brook was sent just in time.

That night after church, Reba Jean decided to make some necessary changes to her schedule. She would keep her mornings sacred to her time with the Lord, gathering her shredded emotions together within the cloak of peace so that she could handle the barrages of each day. She also needed to have the two Velcro dramatists learn they needed God, not just her. With that in mind, she was going to limit her time to reply to their messages.

Her Heavenly Father was still clearly adamant that she was supposed to stay in this job. She trusted that He knew best, so she would draw her strength from Him. She was not going to use the television or food as her escape tool. Even her husband wondered if part of her sleeping problem was too much time on her phone or in front of the TV. That could be a very real possibility. She just wanted her brain to calm down and go numb, so she tried to distract herself with word games or shows.

Reba Jean tried to let this resolve strengthen her, but she felt that familiar twist of anxiety in her gut. It was time to put together the program for the Memorial Service. Her church counselor was going to help her with that. Reba Jean inhaled deeply and wondered where the peace of a few moments before had fled away to. Well, maybe listening to the youth choir CD on her way to meet with the counselor would help.

Chapter 14

Lady Jane had watched the mental footsteps pound through the Library for weeks. She had not seen Reba Jean actually ascend the staircase and come within these hardened walls herself. It was odd, though; the footprints seemed to go into a darker area of the Library, not really to the Whispering Well, and rarely into the treasure room. Lady Jane glanced at her suit of armor and the two Golden Swords and decided that she should go investigate.

Picking up the Oil Lamp off its marble table in front of the Crimson Vault, she followed the murky trail back into the far recesses of the Library. With many twists and turns, the air became stale and suffocating. The misty tendrils were thicker and coarser along this winding way.

Soon, however, Lady Jane was sure she smelled smoke and could feel heat emanating off the walls of this uncharted corridor. Turning what she hoped was the last corner, she found herself in an ancient alcove. In the corner of this indentation of the Library, she saw a middle-aged woman. Her countenance was marred and almost hostile.

The woman looked upon Lady Jane at the entrance and smiled sneeringly. Her eyes seemed to burn with a fire, and the air was heavy with smoky tendrils. Lady Jane felt her armor get hot, and the Sword in her trembling hand seemed about to fall from her grasp. The Oil Lamp did not flicker; however, it just seemed to illuminate the shape of the mysterious woman all the more.

"Well now, just who do you think you are traipsing in here, little girl?" spat the woman acidly. "You have no right trespassing back here; this is MY domain!"

Lady Jane was taken aback, and her eyes narrowed. She needed to be very careful, but neither was she going to back down. This woman, whoever she was, could obviously do a lot of damage to the Library and to Reba Jean. Lady Jane did not even think about herself; she just knew she was no longer just the caretaker or avatar, she was the Warrior Princess of the Library, and by the power given to her from King Abba and Lord Rabboni, she would not back down to anyone ever again!

Slanted eyes that seemed to flicker even more with a glowing fire glared at Lady Jane. The woman advanced closer; the heat emanating from her was stifling to Lady Jane. It did not seem like there was a fire in the alcove, but it seemed as if the smoke and fire were within this woman!

The two watched each other warily, hoping the other would flinch first. Then, the woman seemed to calm down, and she motioned reluctantly for Lady Jane to come closer. Lady Jane gripped the Golden Sword harder and took a step closer. She had been through multiple battles over the years, and this smelled like something conjured up from the Nether Realm.

The woman shook herself and her dark garment changed into a dark red gown with orange and yellow accents. She seemed to take on an almost regal air, but her eyes still glowed dangerously.

"Hello, Lady Jane. Yes, don't look so surprised! I have been back here in this old Library years longer than you have been alive! Reba Jean banished me back here when you came along," stated the woman very matter-of-factly. "She didn't think we should be together, that we might not get along very well."

"What's your name?" asked Lady Jane.

"Oh, I'm Aggie, and before you even bother asking, yes, the Prince sent me to Reba Jean when she was born to watch over her. It's Reba Jean's fault that we have never met," declared Aggie defiantly.

Aggie pulled out a dusty chair that smelled of smoke and invited Lady Jane to have a seat. She began to cook something in a pot in the corner, and the air was permeated with a heavy, cloying scent that made Lady Jane feel nauseous. Off to the side of the alcove was a table full of weird-looking plants and roots. Aggie sometimes fussed over the plants on the table like they were injured pets needing a doctor. Lady Jane wondered if the stuff cooking in the pot was messing with her senses. Her vision blurred, and her tongue felt dry in this overly warm room with its heavy smells and lingering smoke.

Her grip on the Golden Sword did not slip, and she found that if she looked at the Oil Lamp, she could see very clearly. Lady Jane closed her eyes for a second but jerked abruptly when it felt like a burning stick had poked her. She looked to the spot that burned on her arm and saw what looked like an acid burn. It still felt like it was burning its way through her arm! She wanted to scream, but her throat was closed tight from the dryness that was smothering her.

She stumbled to her feet, the Golden Sword dragging behind her. Aggie backed away with what sounded like a cackling laugh. "What's wrong, my pretty child? Can't handle life in the Library?"

Aggie circled Lady Jane like a wild lioness stalking her prey. How good was Lady Jane with that Sword? She knew that Golden Sword and what it was capable of, but she did not really pay attention to the Oil Lamp. Aggie had not heard about the Oil Lamp, so she did not think of it as a detriment to her existence.

Lady Jane saw the Oil Lamp grow brighter, and soon, its light seemed to chase away all the darkness in the room. Aggie was brought into sharp focus through the diamond-etched glass of the Oil Lamp and her sharp features were ghastly to behold.

"Who exactly are you, Aggie?" inquired a very adamant Lady Jane. The light from the Oil Lamp had somehow cleared her beleaguered brain and had brought clarity where the odors had tried to smother her thought processes.

"Now, now, little girl, don't get all bossy and superior with me! I was here first. I belong to the Aggie family, and we have all lived in this Library long before you. My brother, Angus, and my little sister, Angie, are somewhere back there. They pop in to visit every now and again. The Prince has given us authority to live here. You are the interloper!"

Lady Jane was starting to feel that burning sensation course through her. She was starting to wish that she had the water from the Living Fountain or even the water from the Whispering Well to quench the fiery sensations. Aggie, Angus, and Angie, why did they live in the back region of the Library?

Aggie continued to stir the pot that was bubbling over the fire and talk to her strange-looking dead plants. Lady Jane held up the Oil Lamp and looked through it as that seemed to be the only way she could see anything clearly. That one root-looking thing on the table reminded her of something. "Think, concentrate, silly girl," she remonstrated herself silently. That root, what was it?

Suddenly, without warning, Aggie rose almost majestically; she seemed to grow taller and stronger. She took a ladle from the wall, dipped it in the pot, and then sprinkled it over the dead plants and roots. The dead vegetation squirmed grotesquely as if alive. The very air seemed to spark and sizzle, and Aggie laughed triumphantly.

"Oh, how I have longed for this day. It doesn't happen very often; it's almost like having a birthday! Yes, that's it, it must be a birthday!" chortled Aggie.

Aggie grabbed one gnarly root and danced around with it, singing under her breath. She desperately begged this one particular root to come to life even more.

Lady Jane watched in a stunned stupor at the unfolding scene in the ancient alcove. She felt like she was burning with white-hot acid, and the stench of the place was making her almost deathly sick. What could she do? The Golden Sword did not move of its own accord; the only thing that seemed to be of any help was the Oil Lamp. There was no water in this place, and Reba Jean seemed miles away.

Lady Jane felt fear worm its way into her soul. She was on fire from some invisible flame, and she felt sick nigh to death. Aggie seemed stronger than ever, and her very presence was overpowering. With eyes closing in what felt like defeat, Lady Jane leaned her head on the Oil Lamp. The touch of the Oil Lamp felt like cool comfort in the midst of this invisible inferno.

Lady Jane felt her eyes clear again, and she could almost grasp a thought that was trying to work its way free from the mind-sickening stench. The Oil Lamp was trying to remind her of something. What was it?

Aggie continued her ministrations to the boiling pot and the squirming vegetation on the table. She kept transferring hot white liquid from the pot onto the plants, which then seemed to writhe with more energy after each dose. Aggie began a growling cadence as she ignored Lady Jane, who seemed to still be in a stupor. The Golden Sword did not seem too threatening now, and Aggie started to feel invigorated with fierce victory within her grasp.

Lady Jane watched through the diamond panes of glass on the Oil Lamp and soon saw what looked like the poison ivy from months ago begin to take on life, and that odd root over there began to look like Bitterroot! Lady Jane was aghast! She was in the veritable greenhouse of the man-eating plants!

Lady Jane tried to spring up, but the white-hot pain coursing through her seemed to sap all strength from her. The Oil Lamp, however, still burned brightly, and it seemed to cause the Golden Sword to glow. Lady Jane looked through the Lamp at the Golden Sword and saw words from the Ancient One inscribed on its blade as if invisible ink was made visible by the flame of the Lamp.

Aggie stretched out her arms, which had seemed old and flagging, and felt strength coursing through her from top to bottom. Oh, the Prince had not forgotten her! She would soon subdue this wisp of a guardian of the Library, and then she would have free rein again! It had been over forty years of long suffering, but now, at last, she was almost free!

Her family had often tried to run through the Library, and sometimes, they had managed to exert their influence for a short time through the years. This time, however, she did not want to just influence; she wanted to make a huge impact.

Aggie loved that word—impact. In fact, it felt so good to pronounce it that she crushingly smacked her hands together. You would have thought her bones would break with the force of this act. Aggie, with a glowing glare, focused on Lady Jane. Oh, she would love to make an impact on her, for real!

No more than the thought came to mind, then she began to advance towards Lady Jane. She was going to smash her skull against the stone wall of the alcove! That might not make a real impact on the stones, but oh, what an impact it would make on Lady Jane. Cackling like a hyena, she thrust herself towards Lady Jane.

Lady Jane saw the attack coming. She hadn't finished reading the inscription on the Sword, but she thrust the Oil Lamp up as if to shield her from an oncoming blow. Aggie laughed and then stopped as the light from the Oil Lamp seemed to burn through her. What was this? Aggie was used to burning things with her white-hot anger, but this fire felt almost cold to her.

Aggie shivered and squirmed as the Lamp burned steadily, illuminating her very being. Lady Jane, using the Lamp as it was meant to be used, finally clearly saw Aggie for what she was! Her eyes grew big, and determination squelched the lethargy and despondency that had enshrouded her. Holding the Oil Lamp even higher, its rays of light seemed to blind Aggie who began stumbling around screaming obscenities.

The foul language only confirmed what Lady Jane was beginning to realize. There was no way that Aggie was from

Lord Rabboni or King Abba, not with that foul mouth. Lady Jane also had an inkling that Aggie was the cause of a lot of things that Reba Jean suffered from over the years.

Lady Jane dragged up the Golden Sword, and feeling a cold, steady calm come over her, she swung that weapon of divine instruction at Aggie. With a sizzling squelch, Aggie withered into a small, dusty heap of old rags. Next, Lady Jane started chopping all the creepy vegetation on the table, and soon, they were just fossilized dust.

Now, what was she supposed to do with this cauldron of putrification? She couldn't dump it out; she didn't know what would happen if she put the Sword in it. She looked at the Oil Lamp and screwed up her face in a concentrated grimace. She did not have the Living Water here to wash it away. What did she have? A burning Oil Lamp and a Sword, both invaluable tools from the Overseer. The Overseer!

She had the Overseer with her; this was His Lamp and a symbol of His Presence. The Lamp and the Sword: she had exactly what she needed to dispatch this nasty slough of despondency. Lady Jane knocked over the pot with the Sword, being careful not to let its contents touch her in any sort of way. Then she shone the Lamp over the brew. The light from the Lamp illuminated the disgusting slime, which could not stand to be under the light from the Overseer! It shriveled up like a withered old man, soon becoming just a stain on the old stone floor of the alcove.

Lady Jane heaved a sigh, gulped the dryness out of her throat, and surveyed the alcove one last time. She wondered how she would report all this to Reba Jean. Did Reba Jean really know who Aggie was and that she might still be lying dormant to come back to life again in the Library?

Chapter 15

Reba Jean finally had a Sabbath of sorts. She studied Spurgeon and his sermons for a while that morning. Then, she worked on necessary housework. She was able to rest a bit, and she stayed off social media. The TV was turned on for a bit, but she soon grew tired of it. The prayer closet had once again been thoroughly cleaned, and it felt like a major victory. She needed that prayer closet to be usable! She had noticed in her devotions lately that even though the Lord was still affirming that she be still, He also wanted her to earnestly pray.

She had read that the saints of old had spent hours in Bible study and prayer. She did not know how they managed to do this—she had a zoo, ministry, a job, and a husband who stressed her out. In fact, the husband stressed her out more than the job did now. Once she had submitted and taken God at His Word that He wanted her at this job, it no longer stressed her. So how was she going to be able to get enough prayer time in to handle the stress that her husband caused her?

The anger from the other night sometimes simmered below the surface, but she knew she was not to let it control her. The last thing she needed was for that anger to get free rein in her living room or in the Library. Sometimes, she just wanted to bash her head against the wall. The injustice of it all!

Closing her eyes, she willed herself to calm down. The last two weeks had been such a roller coaster. She could say she was going through the stages of grief, except the grief wasn't from her dad dying but from the life he had chosen for her. She was thankful that God had saved her at an early age. She was also thankful that He had put her in a family that forced the Bible and church upon her. It would have been much, much worse if the Bible and church had not been incorporated into their lives. Reba Jean wasn't mad at God; she accepted that He had allowed it. She did not think He had agreed with most of what her parents had done, however.

The memorial service was still two weeks away, and she felt the prolonging of the whole drama wear on her. Her husband, after she had accused him of being more like her mother than she was, had somewhat detached himself from her. Maybe he was trying to be different but did not know how. He still had small outbursts, and she either ignored them or snapped back at him.

He had anger issues, and he couldn't even blame his mother for them! Reba Jean sighed; at least she had been able to write today! Pulling back from her husband and the two women who had consumed her every hour the last two weeks and staying off of social media had allowed her to concentrate on her writing. The devotionals had come together, and she was happy to write two entries! She knew God would give her more in His time.

The day of rest was almost over; she had almost viciously written in book three today, using it as therapy. God had given her a new character to explore, and the chapters had taken shape nicely. Did she dare go see Lady Jane?

Reba Jean paused. No. She was very reluctant to go see Lady Jane. Her avatar would just have to carry on alone by herself and the celestial artifacts. Her mouth felt dry; she licked her lips and felt an odd restlessness. Her day of rest had not gendered much actual rest. She would not get another day of rest for at least another two weeks! She felt panic rush up from her belly; it almost made her nauseous. Everything she had done today, however, had been so very necessary. Tomorrow, yes, tomorrow, maybe she could get a nap after church.

Reba Jean had closed herself within the office to finish a few more pages. She knew she probably needed to go sit with her grumpy husband as he was going to work the night shift tonight. The dryer buzzer going off only seemed to signal that her alone time was over. Would the writing she managed to do today be enough therapy until the next time she was able to write? She still wanted to bang her head on the desk in angst.

Anger, aggravation, and angst, what an ugly family those characters would make. Reba Jean put off going to the Library and decided to check the dryer and try to be nice and sweet towards her husband. Swallowing again, she felt like she had to prepare for battle instead of just going to the other room to sit down.

Lady Jane waited for what seemed like weeks before Reba Jean finally made an appearance in the Library. Together, they sat down near the Fountain of Living Water and tried to share with each other all that had transpired in each of their realms. Their words often overlapped each other, and sentences dangled or tumbled all over. The books clapped their covers together; the misty tendrils looked more like springs bouncing around. Heavy clouds of golden glitter would suddenly explode like a celebration over their heads.

After they both ran out of breath, Lady Jane jerked up and began a strident account of Aggie. Reba Jean listened, and her expression went from frustration to abhorrence.

"My dear, Lady Jane, I am so sorry that you ran into that horrible creature! Aggie is the nickname that she gave herself so many years ago. It is short for Anger, along with her siblings, Angie and Angus, who are both really known as Angst and Aggravation. Together, they are extremely formidable." Reba Jean went on to explain that they were the original avatars of the Library under the direct command of the Nether Realm.

"Well, then, where did I come from?" asked Lady Jane with a quiver in her voice.

"You, my precious Lady Jane, were sent to me from King Abba when I was four years old!"

"Now, wait a minute, are you saying that Aggie was here from the beginning?" Lady Jane was a bit skeptical. Did Reba Jean realize that she was implying that she had been filled with anger from the beginning of her life until she was four years old?

"Just be glad that you did not run into Hattie!" exclaimed Reba Jean.

"Puh-lease! Don't tell me, Hattie stands for.......?" her words trailed off as she looked at Reba Jean's tear-stained face. "I'm sorry, Reba Jean, I wasn't really making fun of something so serious." apologized Lady Jane. It was no laughing matter when someone was full of anger and hate that just the least amount of angst and aggravation could bring those monsters to life.

Reba Jean was so thankful that with the help of the Overseer, those creatures did not control the Library. Every so often, they went on the rampage like the old days, but with the Ancient One firmly positioned in the center and Lady Jane on guard now, those days did not happen as often as they used to.

After a few moments of silence, Lady Jane tentatively asked Reba Jean about the memorial service. Reba Jean shared a few thoughts, mostly about how she wanted to only remember the times her dad had been her champion and how much his face lit up every time they had visited. He always seemed super happy to hear her voice on the phone. Their last words had been, "I love you".

She had been so angry that even with the confession that had brought partial closure, she did not understand why she had had to suffer their choice. When someone had made the statement that he wanted to die with a clear conscience and get that secret off his chest, she understood, but that had not assuaged the anger, only stoked it.

Her husband was concerned that she had not really grieved. She grieved her dad's choices, not his death. She had shed only a few tears; this death was an expected end. She had closure that she had cared for him the best she could, and really, she did not grieve his absence. There had been times here and there where she knew a slight void in her life, but it did not shatter her like when Momma of the Glen had died so suddenly.

Time passed as the two ladies talked together in the now calm Library. Lady Jane chastised Reba Jean for calling KJ and Nellie emotional leeches. Reba Jean understood that it was not very charitable, even if the reality of it was the stark truth.

"You know, my dear, I think I had the Elijah Syndrome," she suddenly announced to Lady Jane.

"What? Oh, I understand. You just needed food and sleep, rinse and repeat?" sagely replied Lady Jane to her mistress.

They continued to sit together, sometimes in silence, other times in snatches of conversation. They discussed RaeAnne and her demeanor at the memorial service. Reba Jean had held a very resentful sister in her arms for a long time that day. She had hoped for further time in person with her, but work schedules got in the way. In retrospect, Reba Jean had wondered if she should have taken bereavement leave.

She watched how people and events so easily influenced everyone around her. How would her dad's death influence her? His life had a huge influence on her, both good and bad. Some things she was still struggling with, so basically, they had a real impact on her. She caught herself chewing off another fingernail as she sat lost in thought there in the Library's atrium.

Looking around the Library, she saw that all the treasure had been piled up and set off in its own alcove. It was a treasure room of sorts, and in there, she saw the Library's copy of the devotional she was writing about that treasure. It was nearly finished, but the thought of that treasure just sitting there, more symbolic than usable, left her unsettled.

Lady Jane saw an interesting expression come over Reba Jean's face, and she began to feel all tingly with expectation. She just knew something in the Library was about to change! She remembered how the Fountain of Living Water had appeared, the Ancient One, the gossamer runner under the Oil Lamp, and the Golden Sword, the suit of armor, and even the Whispering Well all had come to life in the Library. What would her mistress have left to change?

Lady Jane saw Reba Jean look at the treasure sitting there with dull luster and then saw her look at Goodness and Mercy standing there so faithfully. Reba Jean turned her head, closed her eyes, and became extremely still as if she was praying. With a determined air, she suddenly stood up and walked into the treasure room. Lady Jane felt the tingles come to life and realized that something truly significant was about to happen in the Library.

Reba Jean picked up a gemstone, polished it on her skirt, looked at it in the light of the Oil Lamp, and as she set it back down on the floor, it was no longer a jewel but a lovely, beautiful person. Reba Jean did this with every piece of treasure in that alcove. What good was a bunch of sparkly rocks going to do her? She needed her treasure to be alive, active, and easily recognized. Goodness and Mercy had been such integral additions to the Library. What more could Patience, Love, Peace, Sanctification, and the rest do in active form?

She had the Living Word. She needed living treasure from the Word in her Library. The more living treasure she had, the less room for the Hatties and Aggies! Her old sinful self might still be alive, but it no longer had control! The more treasure she had, the more influence they would have in her Library and in her living room!

She reached down, picked up the copy of the nearly finished devotional, and smiled happily at its table of contents. She now had living treasure in her Library, and Lady Jane would have all sorts of companions to help her grow and mature under their celestial tutelage. She had only ten more entries to write as God gave them to her; she felt happily contented.

Chapter 16

Nearly a month had passed since Reba Jean had even been in the Library. She thought often of the celestial companions and eagerly wanted to meet them and get to know them. However, as life always seemed to happen, well, it happened. As she strived to grow spiritually, she felt each battle of wills acutely.

Her husband was going through a very tense time; he even confessed that the root of it was his lack of contentment. Every time she thought she made headway, he would resort once again to his own ways of dealing with his stress—food and spending money. He now seemed insistent that, regardless of the fact that they were in debt and that she was now forced to work because of it, he needed to spend money on cosmetic projects around the house. When she tried to keep her thoughts and reservations to herself, he would prod her for her opinion. She finally gave up trying to get him to see reason. He was bound and determined to spend any extra money they had.

She knew that it was only a band-aid on the internal problem. He had tried to convince her or himself that he was still praying and reading Scripture. However, he was back to some of his old habits. She had to pray harder for him. He knew he wasn't content, but he seemed to think that spending their hard-earned money and eating himself sick was the way to deal with it.

Reba Jean spent hours on the phone each week with Lady Diane as they walked through each of the issues in their lives. Lady Diane had achieved success and victory in the areas that Reba Jean needed help with. Reba Jean knew that Lady Diane had a huge influence on her, maybe even a deeper impact over time. Sir Theo did not seem to approve of the fact that Lady Diane seemed to be counseling her. He also did not like the fact that Reba Jean needed counseling. It was probably the age-old lie that had been perpetuated that counseling is for those who have deep issues.

If there was a treasure of balance, then she needed to find balance. Reba Jean had even begun a Bible study on balance; it mirrored the one that she had completed on being an introvert. Whether she had the Syndrome or APD, or she was just introverted, they all mirrored each other in many aspects.

As time went by, over the month, she wrote many more devotional entries. In fact, after today, she only had one left to write! She was excited, scared, the whole caboodle of emotions!

There were just a few issues with this: she had no money yet to get it published, and what if it wasn't approved by the Emissary of Stone's Corner? There, she stated it aloud. However, she also knew that if God wanted her to write it, He would get it approved and provide the necessary funds!

She felt her hands shake, except it wasn't from her body crashing; it was the sheer emotion of it all. It had been a rough week in this month of rough weeks. However, she did feel more balanced in some areas. She was able to take care of the house, refusing to exaggerate about how much work it was. God kept her safe during work. Nellie was learning how to keep herself balanced; that helped Reba Jean immensely as she mentored her.

Lady Constance was going through a really rough time; she had withdrawn herself from Reba Jean, thinking she was a bad influence on anyone around her because of what she was battling. Reba Jean yearned to have her at least to talk with. Reba Jean did what she had to do; She took Sir Theo and Lady Constance to the Throne of Grace daily, repeatedly.

As this day was nearing its end and the sun was setting, Reba Jean was hoping the Lord would give her a hint on what she was going to lecture the itinerant librarians on in a couple of days. She contemplated a long soak in the tub, but she was too fidgety. Most of her nerves were on edge because Israel had just been attacked by one of the foretold nations listed in Ezekiel 38!

Assuredly, she knew she was to keep writing, but the sense of urgency was so strong. The rapture was imminent; she felt so unworthy, so UN-ready! Her children were either unsaved or so backslid it was tragic, and everyone in her sphere of influence did not seem to even care that Jesus was coming!

Churchgoing was such a social and cultural thing in this region; it had nothing to do with how you thought or lived. Her shaking continued. She looked outside at the sunset and wondered if it would soon be a red sky from bombs instead. What would the people she dealt with every day do when that happened?

She swallowed and could still taste the remnants of the sourdough bread that Amy Lynne had taught her how to make. Its origins were at least one hundred years old. She wondered if the maker of this bread and recipe had even fathomed that people would be sharing it a century later. Her mind was stuck on that number one hundred, whether it was years, devotional entries, or how many ways her husband could drive her crazy.

One hundred years ago, people thought the rapture would happen soon, but at least more of them were ready for it. They had been, hadn't they? Reba Jean found that she thought of one hundred years ago in black and white. She snickered because it was based on the fact that all the photos from that time did not have color. She wished people were more black-and-white in their methods and thinking these days. The world appeared to have gone to the brink of Lot's cities, and it would take a miracle or a storm of fire to rescue any righteous.

Trying to settle her penchant for panic, she had even circled around the house looking to see if she had seen any explosions. She was not trying to be a chicken, but she was a realist, as well. Was there so much apathy that everyone was desensitized? Was it just another war, another battle, another disaster that no one was bothered as long as it wasn't to them personally? She wanted to go outside and yell at the top of her voice, "PRAY FOR THE PEACE OF JERUSALEM!!!"

Reba Jean had a feeling that her husband would have her sent to a padded cell for real. Forget counseling! Or maybe he would wake up, catch the urgency, and cry out alongside her! Would any of her books survive the "Apocalypse"? As much as her books helped her, she truly did hope they helped anyone who would read them, whether now or in one hundred years.

Reba Jean went into a room to isolate and think. It was there that the Lord gave her the topic of her next lecture. It was about the seasons and the spice of life. She was looking forward to the lecture time now that she had her notes ready.

That night as they tried to sleep, they instead began a long overdue conversation. Sir Theo expressed all of his angst, his dissatisfaction, his concern that there was a fine line between contentment and complacency, and his cyclical thinking about his dilemma. Again, no matter what Reba Jean said to try to encourage him, he still seemed to think that he was stuck, at least for the time being.

With her heart in prayer for Sir Theo and for Lady Constance, she also asked for confirmation about the lecture as she always did. In the morning, her devotions were in the same familiar vein: rejoice, sing, and keep trusting God. She thought her body was healing, but on the way to worship, she felt the familiar symptoms arise. However, she just tried to ignore them; she felt like the sermon was exactly for Sir Theo and Lady Constance, and her heart prayed earnestly for them to soak in what God was trying to get through to them. Only time would tell if they let the Word of God change them regardless of the circumstances they found themselves in. The preacher had even mentioned Israel and spoke of the rapture. She was glad she wasn't the only one that had such urgency. She heard that the bombing had stopped, but she had not checked the news today. She just kept a prayerful heart about all that had transpired.

That afternoon, as they amicably made lunch together, Reba Jean knew she would need a nap. Her body was still rebelling physically. Her mind wandered to the Library; oh, how she wished she could go up there. Maybe she could take her nap in the Library? She was so curious about the celestial companions that had been beautiful spiritual jewels. She could picture the lovely, spring green color of Forgiveness; she nicknamed her Fergie. The lush lavender and blush pink of Peace and Love. She knew one of the companions would be arrayed in a lovely pastel yellow; she wondered which one that would be. Oh! Who would be wearing a lovely shade of blue?

With thoughts of lovely hues of treasure, she meandered off to take a nap. Her body did not feel well, but her heart and mind were in a restful state. She sent a few heartfelt thankful prayers up to her Abba, Father.

Chapter 17

It had been a long, wild month. She was still plagued by the mystery malady. The doctor was baffled; however, she noticed continuous signs of improvement. Her church counselor had gone from trying to fix her to herself succumbing to an even worse type of infection. She was scared that Reba Jean had the same thing. However, Reba Jean knew she did not as she did not have the same onslaught of symptoms, and she was also improving daily.

She had made mental trips to the Library, but alas, as always seemed the case this year, she rarely was able to go up there to even check on Lady Jane! While battling for her health and waiting to hear from either the Emissary of Stone's Corner or Lady Dana if her devotional was to be approved for publication, she took on another ministry. Her counsel was being sought about how to be a godly mother. Her heart burgeoned with the prospect, and as she met with this young mother for the first time, she was overwhelmed with the idea that this surely had to be written about by someone already. Reba Jean consulted with Lady Dana, who, in turn, did not have such a resource available.

Reba Jean paused, thought for a moment, and the idea burst upon her that maybe SHE should write such a Bible Study! When this unexpected writing project was green-lighted by Lady Dana, she was overjoyed! Knowing that her third book needed to be finished and that she needed to start on *Porch Ponderings,* she was still extremely pressed to start this project instead.

Thoughts of the treasure companions were still on her mind; maybe someday she would get to make their acquaintance. Hopefully, soon; however, in the meantime, she had to give in to this burning desire to write about godly mothers. She did not even have a working title yet; it would be exciting to see what title God would give her. She was glad He was asking her to base it upon mothers in the Bible because she felt like she did not qualify as a godly mother. But then again, was she trying to make them sound like they were super moms instead of women who lived by faith in spite of failures?

Reba Jean felt a stillness come over her. She wasn't lost in thought; she was just processing everything that was bouncing around in her head. She had heard just that very afternoon that her uncle had passed away. She and Joe Nathan had proceeded to discuss whether or not their uncle was actually saved. Her sister RaeAnne was praising the Lord that the family was reunited in Heaven. Reba Jean did not share that same expectancy. This led to a long spiritual discussion with Sir Theo about salvation, rocky ground, and even the baptism of the Holy Spirit.

Reba Jean, feeling unable to process everything, decided to just go ahead and visit the Library. Maybe there she could settle and organize her thoughts. She wanted to laugh at that idea, but she knew it was true. With a purposeful stride, she ascended the well-worn steps to the Library. She felt flutters of anticipation stir in her gut; she missed being in the Library! Upon reaching the mammoth medieval door, she stopped for a minute. Wait! There were double doors, now, not just a single door! What did this mean? Why was there a full set of doors? The ever-changing door conundrum always mystified her.

Reba Jean ran her fingers over the added door and pondered upon it. She hoped this didn't mean there were two separate Libraries, or one possibly leading to the Nether Realm, and she would need to choose the correct door. She stuck a finger in her mouth and nibbled on the nail. She came close to chewing off that nail as she anxiously wondered which door would lead to HER Library.

Tamping down her worries that wanted to gallop away with her, she firmly grasped both wrought iron handles and pulled the doors towards her at the same time. Nothing happened. Hmm, maybe she was supposed to PUSH, not PULL! It was strange how the door always seemed to have issues of some strange sort over the past few years.

She felt a bit grumpy as, once again, she grabbed both handles and pushed inward on both doors at the same time. With such a strong push, she lost her footing as her momentum and the weight of the doors pushing inward caused her to tumble into the grand expanse of her Library. She tumbled rather ungracefully a few more steps and found herself at the Fountain of Living Water.

Reba Jean inhaled the sweet vanilla scent of the old books that lived in this amazing place. She settled her attitude and looked around. She hoped she would meet the newest residents of the Library. She knew they were avatars of what was to be in her living room. Wait a minute! That thought stopped her in her tracks! She froze! These treasured companions were supposed to be in her living room before they would ever be in the Library!

No wonder it seemed like she would never get to meet them; she had completely misplaced them! Feeling panicked and flustered, she wrung her hands and shuffled her feet. These were to be treasures in the heart, not just the mind. Her gut twisted into a knot, and she felt an overwhelming urge to run to her prayer closet downstairs. Reba Jean was scared that her treasures were not in the living room of her heart but just figments of her imagination.

151

She twirled and ran for the double doors even faster than she had tumbled inside. She never even stopped to talk to Lady Jane or wander around in what she had hoped would be a calming tour of the Library. No, she was desperate to get to the living room and her prayer closet. She had a serious treasure hunt to embark upon. These treasures were not just to influence her life but to leave impacts upon her way of life.

Feeling a scream work its way into her throat, she squashed it down. Her husband would not understand as she had to run past his office, and she did not want to be distracted from her quest. When she had read her devotions that morning, and God had impressed upon her that she should spend time with Him tonight as well, she had no idea that it would be such an urgent necessity.

Reba Jean entered her prayer closet in the living room of her heart. She opened her journal and wrote down the thoughts in her head. Her desire was to find out if she had any treasure in her heart and to be open and receptive to whatever the Lord wanted to show her. She was so rarely in her prayer closet at night. Sure, she talked to the Lord in the nighttime, usually in her bed, but maybe she needed her prayer closet at night as well as at the start of each day.

She opened her devotional by Spurgeon, whose theme was so often centered upon treasure. She read of Christ's alone time with His Father in the Garden of Gethsemane, and the word "companions" jumped out at her. He had companions in the garden with Him, but they were asleep. Maybe her treasure companions were there with her, but she wasn't allowing them to actually do anything but lay dormant. Reading onto the next entry in Spurgeon's writings, she found it was centered upon joy and peace! Her heart winged its gratefulness to her Heavenly Father as He had so quickly shown her the first two companions that He wanted her to get to know.

Overwhelmed by the sudden solution to her spiritual quandary, she hugged thoughts of Joy and Peace to her heart. It really did not matter what they looked like; she just knew how she felt when they were present within her innermost being. She felt such a calmness in her spirit now as she left her prayer closet to go work a bit more on one of those hidden behind-the-scenes ministry of helps that she had started earlier. She did not need recognition or even reward; it was just something that needed to be done, and she was able to do it. In fact, her husband did not even know she was doing it.

Joy and Peace, what lovely first companions! They even hinted at a third that she would not have originally thought of— Satisfaction. Maybe its real name was Contentment. When you have Joy and Peace, you have Contentment, which leaves you more than satisfied.

The very idea that these companions were actually with her, what gifts, what relief, what rejoicing! Reba Jean was overcome with thanksgiving that she not only had treasure in her heart, but she was personally introduced to them. She felt as if maybe she had missed it this whole time, looking for them in her mind but not her heart.

With thoughtful meditation, she finished getting the house ready for bed. She knew she would get a chance to work on the new writing project, but she had a strong inclination that she needed to take care of this treasure hunt first.

The next morning, God strongly urged her to fast and pray for the day. He did not tell her why, but she obeyed. Even later she was not totally sure what the purpose, if any, there had been, except obedience. She had fasted in times past for employment opportunity reasons or spiritual reasons. Lady Constance had asked her a few months ago if she had ever fasted and prayed for her children. She prayed earnestly but had not fasted and prayed for her children. When her doctor had put her on a medical fast for this malady of hers, Lady Diane told her to use it as a time of fasting and prayer. She had not felt that urge then to do such a thing. Fasting and prayer were not something she did ritualistically. She always waited for God to suggest it. There was one thing that happened that night after fasting: She received complete confirmation that God wanted her to write about the godly mothers in the Bible.

She relayed this to Lady Constance, expressing herself with the phrase "totally stoked." That's how she felt, totally on fire about writing. She ached to just lock herself away and write feverishly until all her writing projects were completed. Reba Jean chafed at having to work outside her home, especially with hostile, disgruntled co-workers. Between her job and its stressors and all the outside ministerial obligations, she found herself again questioning God about how to balance all of this. He gave her strength, absolutely, but she really desired to feel more awake, alive, alert, and enthusiastic, and not like a nearly dead hamster flipping around on the hamster wheel of life.

Lady Matilda agreed to pray for her to either find another job or achieve a balance. She suggested that Nellie was probably draining her more than she realized. Reba Jean knew that did often happen, and combined with KJ, it more than drained her. KJ was so much like a chameleon, and that made it doubly hard for Reba Jean to deal with her. Reba Jean had thought that she had been uncharitable in thinking that those two younger women were emotional leeches. She had even felt guilty for thinking such things. However, both Lady Constance and Lady Matilda expressed the same deep concerns that those two were the type that would suck you dry and keep wearing you thin with no chance to recharge.

Reba Jean knew she was going to have to stick to some hard boundaries with those two younger women. "How do you invest in someone..." Reba Jean's pondering came to a halt. All she could hear was the reply, "Don't cast your pearls before the swine." She had heard Lady Matilda say this, and she herself had just said it tonight to another woman at church. She wanted both of those women to not have any excuse for not being shown or taught the right way. However, maybe it was closer to the time to let Nellie walk on her own without so much handholding. As for KJ, she seemed to prefer the lifestyle of sin; her brief profession of salvation had not produced fruit of righteousness, neither had she become a new creature IN Christ.

Sitting at her desk, hoping to write, Reba Jean found herself chewing off her fingernails instead. Sigh, she had felt Joy and Peace the other night, and God had clearly been telling her in the last few weeks to trust Him. However, He no longer used the word "Opportunity" as He had originally with this job. She knew this job was temporary, but it sure seemed to be lasting longer than she had hoped.

Another fingernail was ripped off, and Reba Jean tried to settle her restless mood. Maybe she needed to go back to her prayer closet. Having time alone with her Heavenly Father was such an oasis. These days, He often gave her words to meditate upon that all started with the same letter, or He would give her a theme like "Trust." It was such a thrill to have those words or themes to meditate upon during the long days. Yes, that was what she was going to do: go hide in her prayer closet until bedtime. She would never be able to settle down and sleep with her mind and heart chafing to do things differently than what she was seemingly stuck with doing for such an undetermined time frame.

Reba Jean read a Psalm and then read some of Spurgeon, once again finding comfort in the synchrony of her reading selections. God reassured her that He was not just present with her, but that Jesus was coming soon. She felt herself calming down. She knew that God would help her because He had been doing so every day! His presence was such a present help in times of trouble, a real present. Reba Jean loved the wordplay there—same word but different meanings. Her penchant for being a word nerd helped her to remember easier when it came time to meditate on God's Word.

Chapter 18

Lady Jane sat for a few minutes, trying to catch her breath. These last few weeks in the Library had been the usual roller coaster of chaos and calm. She had enjoyed the additional companions, but she felt like they were not being allowed to actually do anything but sit and look pretty. She hoped Reba Jean would stir up the gift inside of her and let these powerful treasures make a real difference around here.

Sounds drifted towards her, and she knew that her mistress and Sir Theo were getting ready for bed. She could hear fingers on the keyboards as both of them finished up their respective office tasks. It reminded her of the sounds she had heard a few weeks ago that had not been from any keyboards.

When she had followed the sounds, she had been bemused and a bit taken aback to find two books in one of the aisles just jumping around each other. Firmly taking them in each of her hands, she found that one was titled <u>Snap</u> and the other was titled <u>Jump</u>. When she opened them, she read all the snap judgments that Reba Jean had been making alongside her jumping to conclusions. Honestly, there was really never a dull moment in this crazy place.

Lady Jane felt a stillness begin to settle over the Library, and she knew that it signaled bedtime. She yawned and decided to curl up right where she was; she was just too tired to find her bed. The tinkling of the Fountain lulled her into a peaceful dream.

Slowly awakening, she took a mental inventory of the sounds that drifted her way. Being attuned to the subtle nuances of her beloved, recalcitrant Library, she was quick to notice that the master and mistress were not achieving balance. She could tell Reba Jean was striving for calm, and Sir Theo was more about control and organizing what he considered chaos.

Stretching, she felt a nip at her ankles that seemed to come from out of nowhere. There were no dark tendrils or anything to signal that it came from the Library. Snatching her feet up under her, she checked the spot to see if she had suffered any damage. Sure enough, there were two little pinpricks in her ankles.

Moving away from her spot, she perched on the edge of the Fountain and sprinkled some Living Water on her wounds. As she sat there, drawn up in a position of possible protection, she let her eyes scrutinize every visible inch of the Library that she could see. There had been something that inflicted those wounds, and she needed to spot the creature or minion and banish it.

Her gaze moved very slowly and carefully, and after a few methodical scans, she noticed a stirring of air like a little cyclone moving around. It was visible but could also seem to become invisible, depending on the air currents. Listening and watching, she soon discovered a pattern, almost too late, as the biting burst of air lunged at her again. She managed to duck, and it kept on its swirling path. Its destructive presence was visible and dangerous every time her mistress and Sir Theo snipped at each other!

Now, how do you get rid of Snippy? Lady Jane realized that Snippy had been a resident in hiding for a very long time. It would not surprise her if Snippy was the pet of Aggie or Hattie. It was very possible that Snippy and the rats were related, at least by intention. Lady Jane could not fix Sir Theo, but she could help Reba Jean.

With her brows drawn together in deep concentration, Lady Jane worked the problem around, and her only possible solution was prayer. With that thought in mind, Lady Jane moved from the Fountain over to the altar table that held the Oil Lamp in front of the Crimson Vault. Curled up in a ball on top of the table, she began praying for Reba Jean and Sir Theo. However, she felt that maybe Sir Theo needed the most prayer. He always acted like the proverbial bull in a china shop when he was out of sorts.

Snippy cavorted around the Library every few days and tried to stir up bigger trouble. In fact, a few times, he had managed to stir up Angus, who, in turn, snorted and rampaged around the Library. Snippy, feeling very victorious in getting trouble started, began wandering the large expanse of the Library, venturing further and further into the dark recesses where Lady Jane did not like to go.

One day, Snippy decided to go down a long corridor that did not seem to be traveled very often. He did notice that it seemed to have been traversed from the darkness towards the light, but whoever was venturing out of the darkness did not seem to come into the lighted areas. His curiosity was piqued. He enjoyed the antics of Aggie and her siblings; maybe he would find Hattie or some of her kinfolk.

You see, Snippy was not exactly a minion of the Nether Realm, but he had been a long-time pest in the Library. He did not really know of the Nether Realm or its demonic vermin. He did know, however, that the Library was home to some very exciting personages. He loved the rats and even felt saddened when the wild violin and its V's had been vanquished into a sizzle. He had lent his voice to those in the Whispering Well, at least until that had been filled with water from the Fountain. That dratted Fountain really put a damper on him, literally! Snippy just couldn't contain his excitement as he scampered further down the dark corridor.

He did not care much for the celestial companions; they did not taste very good, and somehow, he was not able to nip their heels. Oh, he had tried to drive them away; in fact, he thought he had succeeded in at least driving them into the living room and away from his area of expertise, the Library. However, they soon reappeared again in the Library. That is, in the front of the Library. Back in these dark recesses, there were no Lamps or Swords or companions to get in his way.

The hair on the scruff of his neck began to tingle; he could smell something just up ahead. Snippy began to run; this was an old, familiar scent that he hadn't noticed in the Library as much as he would have preferred! It had the smell of old, dirty rags, and *sniff, sniff*, yes, rotting flesh! Oh! Snippy ran towards the creature in front of him; he could not really see her, but he knew she was there, the smell was so pungent!

Felicia, his long-lost owner, he had almost forgotten about her! Oh! Snippy was ecstatic; he just had to get Felicia to come out of hiding. He knew she would be quite the combatant to kick out those celestial companions and maybe even get rid of Lady Jane. He so wanted Hattie to be in charge; things were so deliciously chaotic when Hattie and Felicia were in full reign!

Cavorting around her, he began to nudge and herd her back down the path she had so often tread towards the atrium. Felicia often tried to get to the inner regions of the Library, but she was often stopped before she ever made much progress. Now, however, she could feel Hattie and the triplets coming to join her from various dark tunnels. It was time to re-take the Library—every book, nook, and cranny!

Felicia felt her power grow, and she was invigorated with whatever was strengthening her. Joining the triplets, they watched for Hattie to appear. However, Hattie did not even come within shouting distance. Well, no problem. Surely, Felicia and the triplets could defeat the measly few celestial foot soldiers.

Arm in arm, they marched in military lockstep towards the light. Surely, the light was just the azure blue from the two windows; it could not be anything more dangerous to them. The Oil Lamp could be avoided or maybe even smashed.

The fearsome foursome, with Snippy yipping and howling around them, arrived at the edge of the atrium. They were ready to advance their cause and return the Library to its original state. As they began to march onward, they seemed to hit an invisible barrier. No matter what they did, they could not get through. They could see Lady Jane and her companions, but they could not seem to do any actual harm to them.

Lady Jane saw Felicia advancing towards her; she was alarmed at the fearsome foursome that lurked at the edge of the atrium. Grabbing both Golden Swords, she stood next to the Ancient One and felt her celestial companions surround her. Felicia looked alarming in slimy rags with venom trickling down her deathly features. Lady Jane shivered, feeling fear trying to snake its way over her. Felicia had never made it this far in a very long time. Seeing the faces of Aggie, Angie, and Angus behind her, and Snippy, like a Tasmanian devil, herding them closer to the Atrium, Lady Jane wanted to scream.

The pages of the Ancient One deliberately began to move, and the Golden Swords seemed to imbue their strength into her. *"Therefore, brethren, we are debtors, not to the flesh, to live after the flesh. For if ye live after the flesh, ye shall die: but if ye through the Spirit do mortify the deeds of the body, ye shall live. For as many as are led by the Spirit of God, they are the sons of God. For ye have not received the spirit of bondage again to fear; but ye have received the Spirit of adoption, whereby we cry, Abba, Father."* Romans 8:12-16. "O, King Abba, thank You," Lady Jane almost sobbed. She knew exactly what to do now.

With a holy war cry, Lady Jane ran towards Felicia and her fleshly forces. Brandishing the Golden Swords, she thrust Felicia and the triplets through, letting the Word of the King be their demise. The fleshly forces could not get through the invisible barrier of grace, but the Golden Swords could easily reach them and put them to death. Lady Jane knew, however, that this might be a frequent battle because the Ancient One had warned her often of such at the words of King Abba. This was the closest that she had been to Felicia and her ilk in a while, though. She truly hoped that she would not have to see her again for a long time.

Snippy did not like those Golden Swords, and the devastation they wrought upon his beloved friends was ghastly. They all retreated backward, stumbling and skulking into wisps of dark, deathly tendrils, just a shadow of the fleeting glory that they had acquired for a few delicious moments.

Chapter 19

Reba Jean sat down to write finally. So much had happened between her Uncle's funeral, dealing with family, trying to balance her husband's volatile moods, and the other stressors of work and counseling others. She had talked to Lady Diane for hours just today, and Lady Diane just kept saying, "Well, that, my friend, is a lot that you have going on."

Reba Jean did indeed have much to process, but she was so thrilled to finally sit down and start typing out her new book. She even managed to write more in the Chronicles series. She was still adding notes for book four, but book three just was not finished. She couldn't wait to see how God would finally conclude it. For a few days, she had wanted to just delete the whole book and give up even writing. Yet, God just gently would reaffirm every day that she was indeed supposed to write and that the theme of book three was exactly what He wanted her to write about.

The title for the book about godly mothers had been quite the dilemma, for all the titles that she could think of had already been used for that same topic. It wasn't until her discussion with Lady Diane that she remembered one that she had used for a lecture years ago, and it seemed that no one had used it as a book title!

The situation with her body's malfunction seemed to be on the mend. A comment made by her daughter-in-law had her running to her medicine box to try a theory. Oddly enough, it seemed to be working! It did not make sense, and it was too deliberate in timing to be a coincidence. She would just see if it kept working this week. Just not having to deal with her body betraying her was a gift, even if for a short reprieve.

Reba Jean sat at her desk as she finished writing for the night. She let her mind travel over all the various things that she had thought she could write about. However, the verse from her morning devotions slid into her thoughts, and she decided to think about that verse instead of the myriad of thoughts. *"In the multitude of my thoughts within me thy comforts delight my soul."* Psalms 94:19.

The Lord had given her joy and peace, she was learning patience and faith, but she still wanted to learn to be still, both in body and in her mind. She could do it for snatches at a time, but she needed more self-control. It would come in handy when dealing with Sir Theo, who, honestly, needed to learn it himself!

A sense of peace and completion fell upon her. She had written like she was supposed to, and she had meditated throughout the day on the Word of God. She felt as if she could go to bed and sleep in peace now. It was so good to not only know what God wanted her to do but to actually do it without excuse.

God would show her how to handle the issues as they arose, and she needed to just trust Him to show her what she was supposed to do. It was time that she stopped borrowing trouble and paying interest on it! With a satisfied, happy yawn, she saved her latest work and turned off the laptop. She had to lecture in the morning, and she yearned for the itinerant librarians to latch onto the Word of God and learn how to grow their own Libraries into places of godly influence.

The week went by, and Reba Jean put some stringent boundaries in place. She worked at making sure that the phone and social media, along with the television, did not absorb her time. She was able to catch up on chores and Bible studies and even started training her brain to be quiet for longer than a few seconds at a time. Nellie and KJ did not understand or like the boundaries that they were placed under, but nonetheless, it had been a much better week for Reba Jean.

It was finally the end of the week and an actual day of rest. She did a bit of housework and gardening, and she then added a few notes to the first two chapters of *Kindly Continue*, her book on the godly mothers in the Bible. She needed to study James 4, as that had been a recurring theme for the last two weeks. She also was ready to delve into a joint study of Genesis with her husband. He was listening to the book on audio and had ordered her the printed version. She had a lot to catch up on, but she was a fast reader.

It was lunchtime, and her bread was still in its rising stage. Maybe she could work on some of those study options. She had a feeling she would eventually study the entire book of James. Her husband kept asking her opinion on things, trying to get her thoughts about his myriad of tasks on his mental to-do list. She was not sure if she would really get to study today.

A couple of weeks went by, or maybe it wasn't that long; it just felt like it. The hamster wheel of life seemed to settle into a routine: the weekly lectures, church, ministries, various Bible studies, the usual cycle of gardening, and housework, along with the ever-present body issues. She had finally concluded that her body was allergic to food, literally. Oddly enough, allergy medicine kept her functioning as her body was designed, in spite of the underlying feeling that things weren't as they should be.

So much of her life felt like a roller coaster. She was striving for that even keel that she thought should be what a good Christian woman should have. Reba Jean had to laugh at herself; just reading Scripture ought to remind her that life was never going to be an even keel!

Reba Jean sat down to write in her book; she might get to the non-fiction book if time slowed down. She had just received word today from Lady Dana that *Treasure for the Heart* had been officially approved for publication. So much joy was shared when Lady Constance and Lady Matilda were told of this momentous occasion. Reba Jean treasured these women of wisdom in her life.

Too many times, she had wanted to scrap book three and just stick with writing about the Bible, but she knew God wanted her personal spiritual journey shared with others, in spite of her own awkwardness and reluctance. Reba Jean sat lost in thought. What would she write about? She could write all day in her head as she worked her job, but when she sat down at the computer, she didn't really know what she should share.

The same recurring themes were still there: Be Still, Submit, Obey, Peace, Contentment, Trust. She highly doubted she would ever move past those themes, just tack a few more onto them, maybe. These were daily battles for her, and so many times, she felt like a failure. Her penchant for fleshly wickedness was very evident; she was well aware that her flesh lay just behind in the shadows, ready to attack in an instant. Her flesh tried to exert its influence in her life, and sometimes, she found it was in control before she even realized it was happening.

"But God giveth more grace...." whispered Reba Jean reverently. It was so quiet in the house at the moment. What a welcome and desperately needed moment of peace. Reba Jean soaked it in, at least until the dogs started barking. She breathed a prayer of thankfulness for even those few moments of stillness inside her heart and inside her house.

No, she would not scrap book three, which she was so close to finishing; she might end up being ruthless in her editing afterward, though.

It was time to check on the banana bread that she had in the oven, calm the dogs, and maybe write chapter three in *Kindly Continue*, her book on godly mothers. Closing her eyes, she tried for just a moment to block out the barking and recapture that moment of stillness and quiet.

Her husband was now home, so she wasn't sure she would actually get to write in the other book. It was getting late, and she needed to get some sleep.

The week went by, and Reba Jean found herself cranky and frustrated, usually at her husband. Her reaction to annoying people was in over-drive. Praying repeatedly did not seem to stop this overly dramatic attitude. Horrific thoughts and suggestions constantly bombarded her mind, and she felt overwhelmed all the time. Was she overreacting? It began to look like the majority of the issue was really her perception or wanting her own way and being frustrated when that didn't happen.

She fought pride, envy, discontentment, anger, and all sorts of battles. By the weekend, however, she seemed to have calmed down, rested, finished the Bible study with her husband, did some housework, and was able to write. On the other side of all that internal drama, she looked back at it and just shook her head. She still was a bit mystified as to why she had had such a reaction to everything.

It was time to finish some letter writing and catch up on other correspondence. Shaking her head again, Reba Jean wandered off to the other room with letters in hand. She was too scared to go to the Library. After a week like this, the place probably looked like a volcano had erupted. Her stomach complained like it had been for the last two months. It was actually better, or maybe just differently afflicted. She giggled at that phraseology, differently afflicted.

Her thoughts meandered down various trails, and soon, the calmness soaked into her. Sir Theo was playing one of his games, and the animals were completely silent and still. It was very cathartic. Picking up a note that she had scribbled on for the books, she was trying to decipher what it said. It had a Scripture reference, something about treasure, and a note to check on something Spurgeon had written. Shaking her head, she wasn't sure she even wanted to straighten out all those trains of thought. Looking around, she spotted yet another note with similar notations for the books she was writing. She heaved a sigh; she had notes all over. Would they ever make it into all the books?

With a bit more attitude than was necessary, she organized the notes and inserted them into the notebook that she was using for *Kindly Continue*. She would figure out what that verse about mothers was for, then switch the notes over to her butterfly notebook for the novels that they seemed to be intended for.

Rubbing her cheek, she settled back down to finish the long letters from Nellie. She would need to write her back by tomorrow and then decide if she needed to respond to any other correspondence. Her calmness felt like it was dissipating. Pursing her lips, she felt silent disgust at herself blossom in her thoughts. Okay, she might be having a mini-Elijah moment; it was time to eat and rest and see if that fixed her mood.

Chapter 20

The first day of fall ended up being the next time that Reba Jean sat down to write anything. The summer had ended with her in a much happier place. Months earlier, she had wrestled with God for permission to quit her job. He had finally given her the date on which she could. She had felt guilty for what seemed like trying to have her own way. However, the date He had chosen surely wasn't the one she had wanted.

As soon as her former boss heard that she was quitting, she immediately asked her to return to work for her. Reba Jean had already told the Lord that if, by chance, the opportunity to return to work in her previous location and position became available, she would never complain about it ever again!

The following weeks had been filled with grueling physical labor, but not once did she complain. She thanked God for the opportunity and second chance to do that particular job again, but this time without murmuring. She had learned so much in the year that she had been working and depending on God to get her through each day.

Reba Jean paused and did a brief mental review of everything that had transpired. How would she even begin to include it all in her book? She had not sat down to write in so long of a time that too much had transpired. She wanted to include thoughts about the new writing studio that her husband had insisted she have. It was her office, her prayer room, her escape, along with her writing studio. It was such a boon in her life; she was so grateful.

The next coming week, they were escaping to the mountains, and already he was setting it up so that she could write while they were away if she wanted to. She took his offer to have access to her books. OH! She also wanted to write about her devotional being available for the public to purchase!

These were the highlights; the other issues were still there. Her husband still had his narcissistic tendencies, although he was working on them. She still was not getting enough sleep, but she was trying not to complain about anything: the zoo, her husband, her health. Her serious health issue had resolved as soon as she quit her job that summer. She still had odd issues that she did not think were related to that. Every time she would mention things to her doctor, he would shrug them off. Now, oddly, a new quirk was becoming an issue. She found that when it came time to write the year in her journal, she would always pick a year in the past, but rarely ever the same year for each entry; it was random. She never started to write the current year. Verbally, she could instantly tell the current year, but on paper, she had to think about it.

Then, just today, she kept having episodes where she got dizzy and had to hold onto something and almost passed out a few times. Would she tell her doctor about those at her appointment in two weeks? Only if they persisted or worsened. She had a feeling it was age-related or from lack of adequate sleep.

Reba Jean's mind wandered away from her current train of thought, and it wasn't long before she found herself in the Library. She giggled a bit. She had not realized that her new writing studio was linked to the Library. She no longer had to climb stairs! This sure was going to make it easier; all she had to do was close out the sounds of life, and there she was, transported straight to the core of her thought center.

With a lighthearted skip, she spun through the atrium, looking for Lady Jane. She had mentally come to the Library to write over the summer, but she had not really interacted with it; it was more like just being lost in thought. That phrase, lost in thought, made her giggle nervously. She knew better than to think such things in this place. She did NOT want to know what "lost in thought" would manifest here in this crazy living center of reality re-imagined.

Lady Jane heard a nervous giggle and the sounds of someone moving erratically through the Library. Pausing to discern if friend or foe, she waited to get a sense or inkling. After a moment, she moved towards the unknown presence. She felt a mixture of anticipation and a tinge of apprehension.

"THUD!" Two bodies smacked into each other, and heads were bumped together. Arms became entangled, and legs thrashed around as the two tried to separate themselves. Holding their hands to their aching heads and trying to clear the literal stars they saw, the two bodies slowly and achingly tried to pull themselves apart. Reba Jean had hit her head so hard that acid arose in her throat. She had been so preoccupied with skipping and twirling in happy excitement that she had not really been looking at where she was going.

Lady Jane felt some tears smart between her eyelids. She felt like all her limbs were intact, but "wowsers," did her head hurt! Squinting through the tears, she tried to figure out what or who had run over her. When things settled a bit, the two looked at each other stunned.

"Who, what, where, how…" their questions bounced off each other, unfinished and full of bewilderment. Staring at each other, they fell into silence. Lady Jane and her mistress had not been together in the Library for nearly four months! So much should have been pouring out of either of them. Reba Jean didn't know what to say or where to start. She should have been here every day or at least every week. Book three should have been finished, and book four well on its way to being done. Lady Jane should never be surprised to see her.

She had allowed her life to keep her away from turning the Library into the place that the Overseer would be pleased with. How could she tell Lady Jane that she was often too scared or stressed or frustrated to spend time with her? Why even her new computer had instilled fear in her, and she had resisted learning how to use it. Yet, tonight, when it was finally time to sit and write, it had not been an issue whatsoever. She hugged herself, but she really should have been hugging Lady Jane.

The avatar, feeling bruised and bewildered, couldn't seem to move towards her mistress either. She had been holding down the fort up here with whatever treasure companions were present or with the Golden Swords. She loved her mistress, but she felt like the Library was more her own place than a place where Reba Jean lived.

"MEOW" broke the awkward stillness. A cat wandered into the Library, one that had never been there before. The two women were startled, and both held their breath while watching this cat wander around. It seemed to be looking for something, and they wondered if they wanted to even know. A second, different-colored cat then wandered in and began stalking the first cat. The puppy followed and watched the two cats circle around the atrium. The Library seemed to have turned into a zoo. The only sounds were the sounds of cat paws walking around.

Lady Jane looked at Reba Jean, almost blaming her for all of this. The second cat wandered out, the first cat hid under a chair, and the puppy began sniffing at its hiding spot. Reba Jean felt more acid arise in her throat. What was the meaning of this, if any? The strange cat started chewing on some trash it had found. That was a good thing, wasn't it?

The puppy came over and seemed to stand guard over the women. Peppy did not trust this new cat, even if it seemed like it was being helpful. Both women rose unsteadily to their feet, and in unison, they escorted the animals out the door of the Library. Turning to each other, thoughts flitting across their faces, but without a word, they both began tending to some long overdue tasks in the Library.

The silence wasn't companionable, but neither was it hostile. It was more like they just did not know what to say to each other. Reba Jean let her thoughts wander, and thankfully, the thoughts were of the imminent rapture. The golden dust motes that responded to these thoughts were like a preview of the celestial.

Lady Jane saw the golden dust motes cascading around Reba Jean and sighed away her inward tension. Any time the dust motes were around, the deathly dark tendrils and minions were nowhere in sight. She knew they would eventually have to talk to each other, but if whatever Reba Jean was thinking about was producing such a celestial resplendent atmosphere, she knew her words were unnecessary.

Working together, they tidied up the place and soon fell into a rhythm like old times. They left everything unsaid, yet somehow, as they worked alongside each other, it seemed as if they telegraphed their thoughts to each other. They had been able to share thoughts silently before, so it wasn't really surprising that it was happening again. Maybe, by not speaking thoughts aloud, they could avoid any reactions from the Library or any creatures that wandered through.

They had a feeling that they were really the two cats circling each other, picking up trash, and playing hide and seek. It did not surprise either one of them if the Library had just illustrated their behavior back to them.

Peppy whined at the door, and Reba Jean rubbed her face. She would not complain; she had promised God that she was not going to be like that anymore. She looked at Lady Jane and knew that, once again, she would need to leave the Library.

However, in the short time that they had spent together, they had accomplished a lot. The Library looked fairly tidy, and the golden dust motes were still sparkling through the light from the Lamp and the azure windows overhead. There was, however, one last thing they needed to do.

God had been telling her of late that she needed to pray more, and what better spot here by the table altar. With Lady Jane, they both knelt and began to talk to King Abba. Pouring out their hearts in silent prayer, the atmosphere soon softened even more. The Presence of the Overseer filled the Library. Beautiful, celestial companions gathered around, raising their hands in praise and honor to King Abba. It was the best way to end such a long separation. Peace settled over the Library once more like a lovely cashmere blanket, velvety soft.

The two women clasped each other in a loving embrace, and Reba Jean once again left the Library. She needed to make sure she came here more often. She also determined that she herself would find a way to have a better godly influence on the Library. She had a feeling that Lady Jane rightly blamed her for most of what went wrong in that place where every imagination felt like reality.

Lady Jane watched her mistress leave again, but she felt like Reba Jean was more resolute and stronger than she had been months before. Turning, she spied the companions that had joined them in worship. She saw more of them this time than she had seen in quite a while. She held her clasped hands to her chest and let the sweet spirit permeate her very being. She had often blamed Reba Jean for all the bad things that happened in the Library; however, she needed to be honest and realize that she was also responsible for many of the lovely things that came into being. Lady Jane might be the warrior princess, but it was Reba Jean who was the daughter of the King!

Chapter 21

"Where to start?" Reba Jean muttered to herself. Her week in the mountains had been better than expected. Her husband had hogged the laptop the entire time, so there was no book writing as promised. The end of the week, however, was very climactic, with floods, hurricanes, driving through what looked like war zones, and finally getting home to chaos and mayhem.

She and her husband rallied the troops and began the clean-up process and taking care of those that they could take care of. Her brother, Joe Nathan, packed his wife and dogs in their car and ran south to the hinterlands. Every time she spoke with him, he sounded like he was having PTSD. There was nothing she could do but listen. Word had reached them that her mother was safe and being cared for as best they could.

What happened, do you ask? It was the storm of the century for this area. It surpassed even the biggest storms and floods that had previously been the talk of legends. Reba Jean was thankful that they had been as prepared and as spared as they had been. This week was full of ordering things that they hadn't realized they should have had in stock.

Throughout the last month, her husband had talked incessantly about the Lord's return, the rapture of the church. With this latest catastrophe and Israel at war with Iran, it sure did look like the trumpet of God would surely sound at any moment. Reba Jean took mental and spiritual inventory. She knew that she was to keep writing until His return. However, she would have to trust Him to figure out the purpose of it. Was it just for her benefit, or would He find a way to get it published and the message out to the masses?

A natural disaster and war surely did have a way of influencing and impacting one's life. It was a test of character, testimony, faith, and integrity when things got hard and scary. Her devotions of late had been full of such counsel for times like this. She knew that God was daily reminding her of how she should conduct herself.

With the rapture surely imminent, it would be easy to just sit down and do nothing. The phrase "occupy till I come" kept resounding in her head. There was a purpose for her to be here, even as weird as that might sound. God wanted "her" here, in this place and time, for His reasons.

Reba Jean rubbed shaky hands through her hair and over her tired face. Tomorrow would commence with more clean up, here or wherever she was needed. Thankfully, she would be able to take a long shower tonight. So many people did not even have water to think of such a luxury.

Her immediate neighbors were all okay, her family was all accounted for, and most everyone seemed to be recovering. Their resilience was wondrous to behold. Her vacation already seemed a month ago instead of just a few days ago. Finding herself holding her breath, she needed to exhale and relax. These were stretching times for her emotionally, mentally, and physically. Spiritually, she had been convicted of not praying as much as she felt she should have been or being the helpmate to her husband that she could have been. She had just finished a study on how to cover her husband in prayer. Sadly, she knew that she could be a better prayer warrior and, thus, a more godly influence on him if she prayed more for him.

Pausing in her inventory, she briefly thought of Lady Jane in the Library. Closing her eyes, she tried to communicate something, anything, to her avatar. After a couple of moments, she realized her mistake in closing her eyes. She was falling asleep! Inhaling and then puffing out an exhale did not make her feel any more relaxed. The Library and its avatar, as usual, were just going to have to make do on their own. Reba Jean needed a bath and bed. She would never be able to keep going if she didn't rest when she could.

Her mind was going a mile a minute, rehashing everything as it always did. It was weird for her to find out that not everyone did this. The term "neurodivergent" kept being bandied about versus "neurotypical." She really believed that those considered "typical" were the ones who had something wrong with them. Thankfully, she seemed surrounded by enough "divergents" of some sort that she wasn't the only so-called "oddball." The terminology did influence her, but honestly, she felt sorry for those who did not remember their dreams or had songs running around in their heads. Even the OCD tendencies actually made her an asset in her particular job.

Being influenced, even impacted by the syndrome, actually had benefits. She would never have believed that just a few years ago. Working hard to overcome what she believed were faults and trying to blend in with so-called "neurotypical" people was less of an issue now. She was aware of things to be careful about and just accepted that she would be this way. The way God made her and allowed her to be to fulfill His purpose.

Putting that thought into writing felt like a personal victory for her. She hoped other "divergents" reading this would understand that their issues could be used for God's glory if they allowed Him to help them. Lady Constance always quoted to her that she was "fearfully and wonderfully made," now she was beginning to accept that truth. God could and did use broken people for His plan.

Sir Theo popped in to check on her and to announce his success on his current project. She tried to encourage him as their conversation turned to why they were both doing these projects. She reminded him it was because God had told them to. He fiddled with some things in her office and asked what she was going to do with them. She offered to let him have them. He acted like his typical weird self, said he loved her, and left the room.

She knew down deep that he did not know what to do with her having her own office or the door closed. It was alright for him to have done that for years; it was an odd feeling to him for her to do it. Her door would never be locked to him, but it would be closed so that she could have some peace and quiet and time to write. He would just have to figure out how to handle that oddity.

A moment later, Reba Jean began to wonder if maybe her husband needed her attention. She wasn't sure if she had missed her cue and his subconscious need. It was time to put down the writing implements, turn off the fan, and go see if she could have a good, godly influence on her husband. She could always try, right?

Attempting to be a helpmeet to a moody man was a challenge. Many times, she wanted to quit—every day at times. He would switch from being loving and sweet to being critical and cantankerous sometimes within minutes. Reba Jean could feel the emotional burnout starting to climax. With resolute purpose to overcome this episode, she went to wash away all her aches and pains.

Like Archimedes of old, this was usually the time she received the most clarity and direction. As her body relaxed, her mind sharpened. She suddenly knew how long book three would be, not all the plot twists or radical edits, but she knew how many chapters and how long those last chapters were to be. It was just the motivational kick she needed. This current book had started to feel tedious when she had not written in it. The scenarios in her head rarely made it onto paper, and that was a personal pet peeve of hers.

The next day, she made chores a priority, trying not to feel like they were a drudgery. The morning stretched out into lunchtime, and her husband decided that he was going to tackle a project he had been wanting to do for years. He didn't want her help, for once. She could tell it was hard for him not to be domineering, but she took him at his word and avoided him and his project.

After a while, she went to her writing studio, turned on a lovely CD of spiritual music, and started writing again. It became a subconscious goal to finish book three and work on the next Bible study book. With her editor on hiatus until the new year, the political situation, and the signs of the times, it felt like the beginning of the new year was the climax for everything. If she could finish all her writing projects, as the Lord gave her the words to say, then she knew she had completed at least one of His purposes in her life.

Pausing to listen to this new CD, she struggled to decide if she liked the style and voices, even though the words sounded good. The song was talking about praising the Lord. The voice and tonality, however, seemed to set her nerves on edge. "This day, I will praise Him…" however did get through the waffling feelings about the tonality. The next song was a bit too contemporary sounding for her liking. She thought about the big debate these days in her circles about song sources versus singers, styles, and even lifestyles. She wasn't going to start an internal argument about the various opinions. She could just hit the fast-forward button on the remote.

The song finished before she could decide to change it. The silence before the next song was a reprieve for some odd reason. Pausing to listen again, the song was new to her, but the words from Scripture were correctly used. Reba Jean folded her hands and tried to let the music soothe her. She loved her writing studio and did not like anything that disturbed its peaceful environs. It was just too much; this CD was obviously just not going to be one of her favorites.

Reba Jean stood up to find music that would fit the praise style that she enjoyed. Putting on an old CD of hymns immediately calmed her jangling nerves. The change was so immediate and radical that it caught her by surprise. Closing her eyes, she lost herself in the sacred words of "How Great Thou Art."

The song ended, causing Reba Jean to open her eyes. She cast her gaze around her writing studio and just basked in its peaceful ambiance. With an unspoken prayer of thanksgiving, she let her mind wander. Maybe she would take a cup of coffee up to the Library and have a catch-up chat with Lady Jane. She felt her body sway gently to the next song. It was so calming and soothing, and her heart reverberated its praise for her Maker.

The whining from Peppy sort of negated that endeavor. "Yes, we'll gather at the river...." these songs were so visual and picturesque, the best humans could do to describe a place they had not yet seen, except through the eyes of faith and the Words of Scripture.

Peppy became more insistent, so together they satisfied whatever her issue was. Making that cup of coffee and sneaking away from the puppy, she made her way to the Library. It might be an interrupted visit as usual if her husband all of a sudden needed her companionship. Hearing a thud behind her as she entered the Library, she turned to see one of those fat cats sneaking in behind her. She watched it warily. It immediately became a nuisance but then crept down one of the long aisles of books. The music could still be heard wafting praises through the atrium. The golden dust motes shimmered in symbiotic waves as if dancing with the music.

The cat came back to rub around Reba Jean's ankles as she turned around in circles to survey the Library. Watching the fidgeting feline, she felt an overwhelming urge to chase it out of the Library. Its yellow eyes blinked at her as it contemplated what trouble it could get into. She nudged it with her foot to distract it from climbing onto the marble table.

It circled her and then sat scratching its ear. Eyeing her with its tail twitching, she felt like the prey. It meowed insistently and demanded her attention. This cat may or may not be trouble, but she really did not want to wait to find out. With an air of indifference, trying to cover her actions, she coaxed it out of the door of the Library and down the hall to where her husband and Peppy were. They could deal with the frisky feline; she was not going to be distracted if she could help it.

Entering the Library once again, the strains of her favorite hymn greeted her with its declaration of "It is Well with my Soul." Sipping her coffee, she meandered around, looking for Lady Jane. Surely, she was somewhere.

The next hymn stopped her in her wandering, and she closed her eyes to listen to it. "Beautiful Savior, Lord of all nations, Son of God and Son of man, glory and honor, praise, adoration, now and forevermore be Thine....". The Library became a sanctuary of praise, and Reba Jean stopped everything to just worship her King of Kings.

A thud against the door startled her; the puppy was locked out. Blinking rapidly as the song finished, she felt her shoulders slump. Just for a few moments, she was transported to the celestial realm, and then she always seemed to be jerked away from it. The music continued, and the whining no longer seemed important.

Concentrating on the words of this next hymn, she tried to recapture the previous moment of total worship and praise. The music was right, but she felt like a balloon that was slowly losing its helium. Her coffee cup was empty, and the snack she had brought was finished. She had not found Lady Jane, but for just a few moments, she had found time with her King.

Chapter 22

The Whispering Well was very noisy lately, and Lady Jane found herself sitting by it like it was an office water cooler in the other world. Sometimes, it seemed as if the Living Water dropped a few levels, and on those days, all sorts of voices could be heard.

Other days, the water seemed to nearly overflow the brim, and it was a quiet, relaxing place to sit. This week, however, even with normal levels of water, she could hear the worried tones of Lady Matilda, the distracted replies of Lady Diane, and the strident or sweet words of Sir Theo. Her mistress sure was going through a chaotic time, or so it sounded.

Lady Jane sat listening intently and could tell by the whispers when her mistress seemed overwhelmed by the many voices that she surrounded herself with. There did not seem to be anything that Lady Jane felt was her obligation to do. She just wanted to stay informed of what might happen in the Library as affected by the outside.

Sitting by the Well, she knew when Nellie would cross the proverbial line, and Reba Jean would have to rebuke her. KJ was rarely verbal anymore. It did not feel like listening to gossip, but it did have an air of something slightly forbidden about it. Lady Jane scratched an itch on her cheek and wondered if maybe she was being too nosy.

Off in the distance, she could hear lovely praise and worship music wafting through the Library. It brought back memories of worshipping together with her mistress. She could hear the whine of Peppy, but her attention was distracted by an odd movement under the water in the well. It was a bit hard to make out, but it seemed as if something was working a hole into the side of the well. Just a little hole, but enough to try to drain the Living Water out of it a dribble at a time.

Lady Jane stuck her head down into the water in hopes that she could figure out what she thought she saw. The movement abruptly ceased, and Lady Jane shook her head and raised it back above the water. This would bear some clandestine spying techniques. Was something truly trying to drain the Whispering Well of its Living Water that filtered all the voices?

Tapping her finger against her lips, she wondered if any of the celestial companions would make good spies. It sounded ridiculous to call them such, almost sacrilegious. She needed Wisdom and Discernment; surely, those would be useful in this situation.

Hearing the pages of the Ancient One flip, she ran back to the atrium to see what message it had for her. That blessed Book had turned to James 1:6, "*If any of you lack wisdom let him ask of God, that giveth to all men liberally, and upbraideth not and it shall be given him.*"

"Well, now," thought Lady Jane, "it says to ask for wisdom!" With that simple, literal thought, she asked King Abba if she could have wisdom. She wondered if this would be a tangible artifact or just something that manifested internally. What would wisdom look like if it was tangible? The Ancient One had so much to say describing the treasure of wisdom. So, if wisdom was indeed a celestial treasure, would it be a living companion like the others or something different?

Meditating upon that thought, Lady Jane went down the resource aisle in the Library. She paged through commentaries and looked at what people defined wisdom as being or seen by others as. She reached a book that highlighted various passages in the book of Proverbs, and it stated that wisdom was like an elegant old lady. Lady Jane almost dropped the book. Wisdom was compared to a "she!" And this particular "lady" had been there when the world was created!

She would love to have this icon of the ages here in the Library, but surely this place was too obscure for such an elegant woman who lived before time ever was! Yet, the Ancient One said to ask for Wisdom... Lady Jane held her breath; her stomach was tying itself in knots. If Lady Wisdom was here, surely the Aggie family would never dare venture out of their devilish holds.

The avatar of this ever-changing Library felt excited, apprehensive, and expectant. Would Lady Wisdom herself actually come to the Library upon the request that she had sent to King Abba? How would she even prepare the Library for such royalty from the Celestial Realm?

The whispering grew louder from the Well even as Lady Jane felt torn between waiting for Lady Wisdom or trying to tend to the issue herself. She had done what she had been told; she had asked for wisdom. Now, what was she to do about the Living Water being siphoned out? If that filter was lifted off the Whispering Well, it was not going to be a good kind of Library.

Crossing her arms, she set her face like flint and determined that she would see this newest chaos through. She was the warrior princess, was she not? With renewed purpose, she decided to tidy up the aisles of books that had gone cavorting around every time Reba Jean had a brainstorm about something.

The first few aisles appeared tidy and maybe even a bit dusty. Nearing the entertainment section of books, she noticed a few of them scattered around. The first one she picked up was that familiar allegory by Tolkien. She knew that Reba Jean and Sir Theo liked to delve into that old saga once a week. She set it on a little stand; there was no point in replacing it on the shelf since it was used weekly.

The second book was a strange book with Sanskrit and English on it. She read the synopsis and a piece of paper that Reba Jean had left in the book. "So full of truth, and yet they don't even seem to realize it," was the note. This book was interesting, but Lady Jane didn't think it was going to be read again, so it was placed on the shelf.

The next book she came to made her giggle; whatever had her two humans been thinking? It was a book on the Japanese tale of Titans fighting. She had a feeling they just needed to divert their minds from the endless tasks that they were doing every day. Were these books having a profound influence or impact on her humans or the Library? Lady Jane had so many questions that it was beginning to annoy her. She looked up and burst into a coughing fit of giggles again. There, above her, the dusty tendrils had formed themselves into question marks above her head.

Walking through the rest of the aisles took no time at all. She neared the end of all the rows that were usually used, and a faint sound caught her attention. Turning the corner, she saw some bookshelves just beyond the atrium in a dimly lit corner. A few books were scattered on the floor there, and she went to tidy up that seldom-used section.

Picking up a book that she had never seen before made her curious. It was a historical account of the area that Reba Jean had grown up in. Little country towns in a quaint corner of the map, full of the usual tales of church, school, community, families, and commerce. The book felt odd and tingly in her hands, and she set it down. Nearby was another book; it seemed to be a chronicle of all the places that Reba Jean had lived. That book, too, felt odd to the touch.

Mystified, Lady Jane stood still, not touching either book but getting a sad sense from both of them. It wasn't quite pity, but it was a sense of wanting to belong somewhere. Lady Jane understood, for she herself was acutely aware of all that her mistress had gone through. That feeling of nobody wanting her, truly loving her, and not belonging anywhere.

Louder whispers from the well seemed to wrap themselves together with this cloak of melancholy in the dim alcove. Lady Jane wasn't aware of any danger; she was just caught in the mood of wishing that, just for once, she and her mistress were loved and accepted for the way King Abba had made them.

Felicia had figured out a strategy to subtly return the Library to her control. At least, that was her intention, as she slowly siphoned out the Living Water in the Whispering Well. She was very careful not to let that celestial-tainted water touch her in any way. She just very carefully created a channel in the wall of the cistern about the size of a coffee stirrer straw so that the water level decreased incrementally.

Her efforts were rewarded daily as the voices became a mixture of complaining, murmuring, anger, and frustration. Every so often, she would whisper her own suggestions, such as, "You don't have to put up with this; you can just leave!" And much to her satisfaction, she heard Reba Jean confess this very thought to both Lady Diane and Sir Theo and then even to Lady Constance!

Felicia did a hoppity-skippity dance, twirling with self-righteous glee and pride. She skipped up the back staircase, which no one seemed to know was even there, and there she had a bird's eye view of Reba Jean's world. Here in this unknown lookout, she could scope out and find things to slyly suggest from this vantage point in the Library.

It was from this vantage point that she saw Reba Jean packing a backpack! Was this how this marriage would dissolve? Oh, with that unholy thought, she ran all the way to Hattie's hovel in the dark, recessed caverns of the Library. Sitting around Hattie's smoky, sulfuric stove were Angus, Angie, and Aggie. With glee, she began to tell what she had seen, knowing that Hattie would love this tale of woe that she was spinning. However, Hattie cut her off with a curt question.

"Did she pack any toiletries?" Hattie barked.

"Well, no, not yet. She only packed, well, one change of clothes so far," stuttered Felicia under the full glare of Hattie's rancor.

With her standard scowl, Hattie cackled something unintelligible and then said, "Keep at her, but be careful; this may be something completely different."

Aggie looked thoughtful and stated that there was a rumor that they were preparing for the end of the world or something. The triplets only heard rumors from their end of the Library, so everything was often distorted or half-truths. These half-truths had a life of their own, however, and often ran through the Library unchecked to their devilish delight.

The rumor that Reba Jean had been kidnapped by a serial killer and that she had allowed Sir Theo to be shot so that she could escape had swirled around the Library for a few days. They even heard Reba Jean talking about it. Of course, her voice and the retelling of it was obscured by distance, but surely it was something along those lines.

The triplets began fussing and arguing amongst themselves, as was typical of them. Felicia fumed under Hattie's rancor, and Hattie just sat stirring her own pot of bitter herbs as they spurted and boiled over into the sulfuric flames. Hattie enjoyed stirring her putrid pot of bitterness, anger, rage, malice, and discontentment. She might be way back in the recesses of the Library, but she knew that if she kept that pot boiling, some of the contents had a way of oozing into the main areas of the Library, even if by circuitous means. That shield of faith would still need to be dealt with, along with those Golden Swords and that wall of grace. Albeit, the long game was what the Nether Realm had taught her, and she would just bide her time.

Hattie did not want Felicia to get all the victory, so she downplayed her story of Reba Jean's packed bag. There would be no quiet if Felicia thought for a minute that she had been the purveyor of the catalyst. Hattie wanted some credit or all of it; she was the menacing mistress here, wasn't she? She turned over the news, and what Aggie had stated—world ending, marriage ending, sanity ending—all sounded wondrous to her. Now, how could she further any or all of these along?

Chapter 23

The weeks bled into each other, a roller coaster of emotions, defeats mixed with victories, back to defeat. Reba Jean was lamenting that she had no consistency, just the constant hamster wheel. Some days, she had wonderful spiritual growth, and other days, she was ready to just quit and run away. She had confided in Lady Diane, who suggested she (and her husband) get real professional Christian couples counseling.

When Reba Jean told her husband, his answer was silence, and then he changed the subject. With her heart crying out to God for help and an answer, He had told her that she needed to stay and not run away. So once again, she gathered her shredded emotions and hurt feelings and attempted to find a way to put up with her husband's narcissism and fits of frustration.

She truly believed that he had mental health issues, but he wore his shortcomings as a badge of honor. Looking around at the other men that he fellowshipped with, most of them seemed to behave in a similar fashion. Both Lady Matilda and Lady Constance were having similar issues plaguing their marriages. Were all men like this? The Scripture was so very clear on how marriages were to be according to God's instructions. Yet, it seemed like it was only preached on how women had to be subdued and obedient, and if there was a problem in the marriage, it was most likely because the wife wasn't being obedient. Reba Jean shook her head; somewhere between the preaching, the reading, and the applying of the same Word, it got all twisted.

Basically, because of Eve, women shouldn't be allowed to be everything that God had designed for them to be. Oh, Reba Jean knew that sounded harsh, but she couldn't seem to see how any of the men in their sphere proved that statement to be inaccurate.

No, she wasn't leaving her husband; she was, however, no longer acknowledging his fits of anger or trying to assuage them. She was definitely not getting in the way or trying to fix it. If he broke things, that was on him.

During his last fit, he kept looking at her, expecting her to react like she always had. She looked right back at him and let him act like a toddler. The rest of the night, he tried to act as if he hadn't behaved like a jerk. He tried to be sweet, and his eyes said he knew he hadn't behaved right. However, as usual, he felt justified for having a fit over very petty things. When she mentioned his fit a few hours later, he justified his behavior like he always did.

She wasn't sure if what she had was PTSD, but she probably had her own version of it. Her husband was so much like her mother that she felt as if she could never truly heal from the hurt of her childhood. She even started a devotional about how to heal. She had not gotten far into it, and it did not seem to touch the inner hurt yet. Maybe it would by the time it was completed. She was searching for that help to heal.

She honestly did not want to talk to a professional counselor. Not if her husband wasn't going to get help for himself. You can't help someone who doesn't see anything wrong with their behavior. He had grown up surrounded by couples who yelled and fought all the time. She had too, but she did not want that. He seemed to think it was normal and to be expected since no one ever did anything to his satisfaction. Even if they did, it never lasted long.

The hurt was still there from when he said he did not want a copy of her latest book. He had no plans to read any of her books. She finally told him not to bother reading them; they would only make him mad. He supported her writing; he often encouraged it, but he had no desire to see what she actually wrote.

His life was a series of frustrating events, and since he was never content, it would seem that he would always be frustrated by everything and everyone. How could anyone even enjoy life if they were easily angered by just the littlest thing? Reba Jean just did not understand people like that or even how to live with someone like that.

After talking with a very despondent Lady Constance, who was suffering her own defeats, they covenanted together to pray daily at a specific time for each other. They both set alarms so that they could stop and pray earnestly. Consistency was a constant battle, so Reba Jean really hoped that this would be something that would last the rest of their lives and not be a short-lived plan that fizzled before it became a habit.

One day, Reba Jean talked with her church counselor and confided that she was a published author. They were discussing how Reba Jean felt like she was always considered a weirdo. The counselor interrupted her to exclaim what skills Reba Jean had in counseling other women, teaching the Bible, and being an amazing cleaner and organizer. She said being a writer just made Reba Jean a really cool weirdo.

A few days later, her boss came to her and said that she was trying to be like Reba Jean and not complain. However, she had not arrived at that point. She had a meltdown and seemed to feel sad that she couldn't get to the place where Reba Jean had finally gotten.

Reba Jean tried to find comfort in the fact that she was having an impact on people and was a good influence on the women around her. Most of them did not even realize the battles she fought almost hourly. Neither did they have a clue how very tired and exhausted she was. However, she had learned that a symptom of the Syndrome was chronic fatigue. With that possibility, she realized that she would always feel tired.

On a happier note, she was going to schedule a lunch date with Scarlett, a possible new friend. They were kindred spirits, and she hoped they would be able to spend more time together. Lady Dana had introduced them and thought they would have much to talk about due to their similar childhoods.

Reba Jean had also found another possible kindred spirit in her new dental hygienist. They were talking about Reba Jean's dreams, and Ann told her she should write about it! Reba Jean had to giggle to herself until she told Ann that she did indeed write about her dreams!

Her spirits lifted just thinking about it, and then her husband said that she should spend more time with Lady Constance. They had taken a road trip together just this week, and it had been wonderful! They planned a day to spend together next week as well. Reba Jean was really excited. Yes, they had their shared troubles, but when they got together, it was such a time of animated fellowship and discussing God's Word. Reba Jean fully expected them to be able to pray together as well. Oh, how thankful she was for Lady Constance.

She really needed to call Lady Diane back. They had not had their weekly session, just some texts back and forth. It seemed like Lady Diane only got to hear how bad everything was in her life. Would there be a time when she could share good news with Lady Diane instead?

Peppy was whining as usual, and her husband was adamant that it not bother her. She was grateful that she now had her own studio and could close the door. He, at least, had given her that escape. She loved her little oasis, although she knew he would probably come in shortly. He seemed to need her to be attentive to his thoughts and ideas and plans. She felt her stomach churn and felt stressed as soon as he drove into the driveway. Her health tracker said that the only times she had high stress was directly related to interactions with her husband.

Rubbing her eyes, she realized that she had not even been to the Library. Her eyes started twitching, and her stomach wanted to heave. It would do no good to go to the Library while she was stressing out. She tried to exhale and calm down. The devotional books near her seemed to beckon to her silently. She needed some good Bible Study time. That's what she would do. Maybe that would settle things down in her mind, heart, and body.

If she had thought about it, she might have realized that all of this was a huge spiritual attack. Somewhere in the back of her mind, she knew it. However, it did not seem to flash warning signals like she would have hoped it would. Bile rose to her throat, and she felt the acid burn. She was super stressed just thinking about all that had happened in the last couple of weeks. She was going to have to dig into God's Word, but the puppy was whining outside her door again. She popped an antacid in her mouth, grabbed a peppermint to settle her stomach further, and went to get lost in the writing of men like Spurgeon and Havner and the prophet Isaiah.

Her reading took her to Isaiah 53, and she began to cry. This chapter was all about what Jesus had felt and suffered for HER and her sin. He knew exactly how she felt and what she was going through. He also knew her innermost thoughts and the sin that so easily beset her. That sin was what He took upon Himself—for her! He did know; He did care! As was her typical reaction, she always found something that she wanted Lady Constance to hear. Lady Constance needed Isaiah 53, too!

Spurgeon changed her perspective from "woe is me" to "How wonderful is He?!" Then, it reminded her that she needed to have faith; she had felt so lost and had begun to drown in her emotions. Her devotions began to pull her back from the abyss that she had sunk into.

Havener reminded her to have FAITH and gave her acrostics for that word. For all she needed, for Who He is, she was to thank Him and trust Him. He is the Christ of the lonely road, and it brought her full circle to Isaiah 53 again. She opened the next devotional book that she nicknamed "Bread." It used the very word covenant and reminded her that her marriage was a covenant, not a contract. It was to reflect God's love and light, and when she reflected God's love, she would be able to love and forgive her spouse. It urged her to pray for her marriage.

Every time she needed something, God always gave it to her. She felt the hope surging in her soul again; she had a couple more devotionals to read tonight. What else would they tell her that was so sharply on target she could almost feel the prick? Reba Jean picked up *Streams in the Desert,* and the words were a sweet but instant call of correcting from her Shepherd. It reminded her of the book *Hinds' Feet on High Places*. The emissary of Stone's Corner had compared her own writings to this book. She had never read it and had been really scared to. However, Lady Matilda had given it to her during the summer, and she had read it. With sheer amazement, not only did she have the same writing style, but much of what she personally felt and struggled with was written down in that allegory. The emissary was so accurate when he had insisted that her books and life were like that wayward, scared little sheep. Now, as she had read Isaiah 53 and her devotionals tonight, she felt again that she had slipped down the mountain into the swamp instead of kicking her heels up on the highest parts of the mountains.

She had one more devotional to read for the night, well, except that one about healing the hurt. She wasn't sure how much more she could absorb; she was trying to take it all in. She wanted more out of her devotionals, so she read at least five different ones and more than just an entry in each. This had really filled the void that she had been feeling for wanting depth and spiritual food. She could feel the answers and hope mending her shattered heart back together, and the threads of despair felt like hugs of hope. In the last couple of weeks, she had only gotten in Scripture reading and not the extra devotionals. She did not realize how much the Lord used them to speak directly to her needs until now, when she had gone without them for so long.

She would need to fight for her time in Bible study, prayer, and reading these balms of Gilead. She had been drowning and had not really needed to be. The help and hope had always been there; she just hadn't dug the ditch in faith and waited for God to fill it. She really wished Lady Constance could get the same help and hope. She would send her the devotionals, but she had a feeling that maybe Lady Constance didn't truly want help and hope. She just wanted to quit. Lady Constance had succumbed to one of her dark episodes.

Reba Jean sucked in a gulp of air and went to finish the rest of her reading. She wanted to sink to her knees, put her face on the ground, and pray to her Heavenly Father about all of this. In fact, she could do that right here in this precious prayer closet if she would just take the time to do it. Time passed, but she felt like it was standing still as she poured her heart out to God, asking forgiveness and thanking Him for helping her and reminding her Whose she was.

Her stomach was no longer churning; she felt cleansed and more settled than she had felt in a very long time. It wasn't self-determination but spiritual grounding that steadied her. She blew out the last few breaths that she felt like she had been holding in for so long.

It was time. She needed to go see her husband and not be deterred from being the wife that God wanted her to be, regardless of what her husband was acting like. She answered to God, just like he would. She wanted to give a good account of how she had upheld her side of the covenant.

Lady Constance would need a good influence in this area as well and a good example. If Reba Jean had any impact on Lady Constance, it would need to be in the spiritual arena so that it would affect the mental, emotional, and physical. Reba Jean had been praying for Lady Constance all night; she was not going to wait until their appointed time the next day. Lady Constance needed a prayer warrior right now!

Girding the loins of her mind and calming her fleshly reactions, she gathered her thoughts so that she could be civil and attentive to her husband. Her flesh wanted to rear its ugly head and tell her she didn't need to act upon what God had told her. It was too soon; she was too raw and hadn't fully healed.

There was no need to go into battle while she was still recovering.

There was no need to listen to the doubts; they weren't warnings. God had given her all that she needed to survive and thrive. It was time to act out in faith what she had read and prayed. Maybe she could be a good influence on her husband—maybe.

Chapter 24

While Reba Jean was grounding herself back in the Word of God and renewing the right spirit of her mind, Lady Jane had her own issues to deal with in the Library. The hair on the back of her neck matched the quivering of the Golden Swords any time they went near the Whispering Well. There was definitely something afoot with the water level. Even when she poured in more Water, it seemed to slowly seep out somewhere.

Lady Jane began rummaging around in the unlocked chests and strongboxes, looking for anything she could find to figure out how to fix the leak. She had not run into Lady Wisdom in a visible form; however, she felt stronger clarity and discernment about the Whispering Well than she had before when she let the voices lull her into lethargy.

Passing through a well-used aisle of books, she noticed that Reba Jean had been busy writing again, taking notes, and walking through her devotional books. That was a relief; in fact, the observation made Lady Jane stop in her tracks. She had a niggling of a thought as if a misty tendril had tapped her on the forehead. She looked up, thinking maybe one actually had. No, they still hovered overhead like so many will-o'-the-wisps. The term she thought of to describe them seemed so accurate; they were wisps of willfulness.

In any other Library, they might be ghostly lights, but praise be to King Abba, here, they were just thoughts waiting to be willed into action.

"Okay, so if whatever Reba Jean did directly affected the Library, and something had sprung a leak in the Whispering Well to let in ugly voices, then…."

"Well, then, maybe this aisle of books she was in, which was once again back in use, might be a direct correlation." Lady Jane turned around the thoughts in her own head, not trying to voice them audibly until she had them sorted. Was there something in this aisle of books itself that would find and seal the leak?

With a plop, the wise little avatar settled down in the middle of the aisle to carefully peruse the books around her. She saw *Morning and Evening, Bread for the Journey, Streams in the Desert, My Utmost for His Highest, and All the Days,* along with the Blessing book and the prayer journal, and Reba Jean's daily notes on what she read from these books. With chin in her hand, praying for wisdom to guide her, she looked further around behind her. Hmm, *Submerged* and *Castles* and *The Rescue* looked appropriate. *Every Storm* and *Leave a Candle Burning* also appealed to her. Another set of books were Reba Jean's own novels about the Library being full of secrets turned into treasure.

What could she do with a castle full of treasure when what she needed to find was submerged in a well? If she went into the well, would she need to be rescued? "However," she mused, "the water is the Living Water; how could that possibly drown me? I will just leave a candle burning at the top so that I know which way is up," she surmised.

The little song "This Little Light of Mine" began running through her thoughts and out of her mouth. The golden notes from the music room danced merrily over her head, lighting her way as she went to find a candle.

Felicia got tired of being under the domineering glare of Hattie and the terrible triplets, and she flounced off to her own little alcove in the middle of the vast Library. Whether or not the rumors were true, or whether Reba Jean left Sir Theo, only time would tell. Meanwhile, she had her work cut out for her. She needed to finish draining the well so that she could speak her own truth and feelings into Reba Jean's subconscious.

She would let Hattie stir up the hate; the triplets would stir up the aggravation, angst, anger, and agitation. She would just come by and soothe her with thoughts of taking care of herself. The emphasis on self, of course. Felicia, after all, was the fleshly side of Reba Jean's psyche.

As she found her own little, dark, fetid alcove, she felt a huge yawn escape from her pouty lips. Well, maybe she had time for a nap. It must be Sunday; she only seemed to get really tired on holy days when Reba Jean was stronger spiritually and her flesh seemed to be under some sort of control.

Felicia curled up to take a nap, not knowing that her shenanigans with the well were about to become a battle of wills. If she had any wisdom, she would have been on guard instead of sleeping. However, since she was the flesh, the flesh is prone to be ignorant and self-gratifying.

Lady Jane felt a yawn escape; she knew it was a day of rest, and she should be resting. She knew that Reba Jean would be trying to rest for a bit on this holy day. She glanced at the large clock suspended in the cathedral-style ceiling and calculated how much time she had to prepare her tools for this project and if there would be time to rest.

She needed a waterproof candle that wouldn't blow out or be snuffed out, she needed something to seal the hole with when she found it, and she needed a way to safely rappel into the Well and back up. A threefold cord would be best and maybe a candle dipped into the Oil Lamp, but what should she seal the hole with?

She did not have the answer to that last question, and she felt her eyes closing into slumber as she slumped down on the marble table holding the Oil Lamp. She would need to sleep on it, or so it would seem.

Hours or minutes passed; time remained wonky in the Library. Lady Jane awoke feeling an odd sense of rejuvenation. The Library was humming, the music room was up to full volume with lovely worship music, and the whole atmosphere seemed to be one of praising Lord Rabboni.

With only a moment to gather her scattered thoughts, the little avatar of this massive Library realized that today was a very special day! No, she had not found a way to seal the leak in the Whispering Well, but there were other matters to attend to.

With golden dust motes quivering around in glittery excitement, Lady Jane ran through dusting all the artifacts, hugging all the Celestial companions, and lovingly touching the pages of the Ancient One. She polished and sharpened the Golden Swords and made sure the Shield of Faith was still as strong as ever.

Running down the aisles, she replaced wayward books, checked locked strongboxes, and tidied up the atrium. With her hand, she splashed Living Water on herself and then mopped the floor with it from that lovely Fountain in the middle of the atrium. With great speed, she ran up the circular staircase to the azure windows and looked out. Sure enough, her mistress was also celebrating this wonderful day. In fact, she knew her mistress would be coming on this day of all days, for real, to visit the Library.

Lady Jane visited the hidden portico, ran down the hallway of hope, and threw some more water into the Whispering Well. With a song of praise bursting forth from her lips, she ran back to the Ancient One and waited with great anticipation.

Without fail, the lovely pages of Scripture opened up to the Gospel of John, and Lady Jane hungrily read chapter after chapter of this precious book about Lord Rabboni and His life and ministry when He was on the earth. This day was very special to her and her mistress. This was the day when they commemorated how Lord Rabboni told Reba Jean that she was a sinner and needed to be saved. That little girl had felt such conviction that she crawled under her brother's bed and gave her heart to the Lord. He forgave her sins and made her a new creature to live for Him and serve Him for the rest of her life.

On that day, the Library gave birth to a new avatar, Hattie and Felicia were banished to the back, and Lady Jane was born! That had happened forty-eight years ago on this date! Lady Jane was fervently thankful to be alive. Over the years, she had suffered much with her mistress, but through it all, the Lord had been so close and had carried them both through every issue. Now, all these years later, they were actively working on keeping the Library clean and pleasing to the Lord. The Overseer was there to guide and comfort them.

Captain Insidious and General Nefarious did not seem to be around much lately, at least not in person. They did seem to be connected to Hattie and Felicia and their ilk, though. She knew that she still had to figure out how to fix the Whispering Well. However, by faith, the answer to that problem would be given to her.

Bowing her head to the floor, she gave thanks to King Abba for Lord Rabboni and His gift of salvation. She thanked Him for the Overseer and for all the artifacts in the Library. She named each of the treasured companions by name, and then she prayed for Lady Constance and all those who had an influence on her mistress. She then prayed for Reba Jean to be a godly influence on everyone around her, as well. When she ran out of words, she just stayed in place and soaked in the sweet stillness of being in the Presence of her Lord and Master.

In just a short while, she felt a sweet hand grasp hers, and with a smile on her face, she was joined by her mistress, Reba

Jean. Together, they continued to pray, worship, and read the precious words of the Ancient One. It was a lovely time of fellowship and celebrating their new birth together.

After some time had passed, Reba Jean began to look around the Library, noting how clean and organized it was. She thanked Lady Jane for keeping everything ship-shape. They giggled as they ducked just in case a ship came sailing through overhead.

Reba Jean shared that she and Sir Theo were preparing for a critical time in their lives. Persecution would surely arrive, and they were working towards doing what they could to prepare for the next few years or less before the Rapture.

Spying the threefold cord and the candle dipped in oil, Reba Jean sent a questioning look toward Lady Jane. With great animation, the avatar explained the situation and her dilemma. She needed to keep the filter of the Living Water in the Whispering Well. It was slowly seeping out somewhere, and Lady Jane just couldn't figure out how to seal the leak.

Reba Jean pulled a new book out of her pocket; it was on how to turn your house into the safest place on earth. It had been written by a Navy SEAL: surely someone like that knew how to deal with leaks and how to seal up holes.

She skimmed through the table of contents but did not see anything that seemed to speak to the issue in the Library. However, she saw much that she needed to show Sir Theo, so with a hug and a promise to pray about the Library situation, she bid her sweet avatar farewell and headed back down to the living room.

Lady Jane watched her mistress leave, knowing that it was important for her to connect and communicate with Sir Theo about this book and its information. She was a tad disappointed that they had not reached an agreement and a plan of action to fix the well. She refused to let any fleshly emotions or disappointment cloud her perspective. Today was a good day, a godly day, and she would not let anything change that.

Lady Jane spent the next few days feeling like she was so close to the solution, yet it just seemed to be floating in the ether of the Library and not presenting itself in a tangible form.

She had a wonderful interlude in the midst of all this to go on an excursion with Lady Constance, Skye, and Daisy Mae. She listened in from the Library as Reba Jean counseled and guided Lady Constance through Scripture, addressing their marriages and issues.

She felt how acutely aware Reba Jean was of the fact that even her silly side was an influence on the other women. Lady Jane felt that sharp tug as Reba Jean wondered if she should have been more sober or serious during the time together with the impressionable girls.

Lady Jane enjoyed her time off from Library duties that weekend as Reba Jean took time to recharge and rest. She sat back, surveyed the Library, and took a mental and visual inventory. It didn't take long, though, to see a new thought had formed and just kept peeking in and out around the books. Lady Jane looked closely at the thought and evaluated it. Intrigued by its appearance, she stood up to get closer to it.

It was a recurring word that kept popping up in Reba Jean's Bible study of late. The word was "covenant," and once it appeared, it just kept reappearing randomly. As with any thought or word that wanted to take root in the Library, it had to pass inspection. However, since this word came straight from King Abba, there was no concern about its value.

"Covenant," whispered Lady Jane to herself. That word just seemed to hold extra weight and value. With eyes wide in wonder, she began to consider if it was a new treasure for the Library. "OH! What if this thought, this word, becomes a companion?" she half-exclaimed aloud.

Then, as if the Overseer had whispered straight to her heart and mind, she jumped up, grabbed the word "covenant," and raced to the dictionary section of the Library. Flipping through multiple dictionaries with excitement, she read the different meanings of this word and its uses. Dropping the dictionaries and clutching the word "covenant" with its meaning of a "bond," she raced to the Whispering Well. A bond, a seal, a promise that can't be broken, this was the perfect word to seal up and bind the hole in the well! Call it a bit unorthodox, but it was the Library, after all; it was the exact sort of thing one would expect to happen!

Without fear, Lady Jane jumped into the well, felt all around the wall, and, after her frantic searching, calmed down to begin a very methodical inspection. She finally found the hole that Felicia had drilled into the wall. With great care, Lady Jane covered the hole with the word "covenant" and watched it form a tight, unbreakable bond over the place where the fleshly side of Reba Jean had been draining out the Word filter.

Chapter 25

Reba Jean had been very subdued since the last conflict with Sir Theo. She had struggled to be more consistent in her Bible reading. The distractions still came, and sometimes they did deter her from real study. She, however, had been convicted to be the wife that God wanted her to be regardless of how her husband acted. She was accountable to God for her words, thoughts, and actions.

Her husband kept looking at her as she was either softly agreeable or very quiet. He seemed to realize that she was unsure of him. It always felt like she was starting all over again after one of his fits or tantrums. This weekend, however, after she and Lady Constance had agreed to work on their own relationship with their Heavenly Bridegroom, she knew it was time to let the pain and hurt and scars heal and try again.

Her heart was still a bit steeled against getting hurt again, but she and Sir Theo seemed to be back to a loving bond. God had granted mercy in the last week to their nation and maybe was granting more time before His return. She still wanted to finish writing all that He had laid on her heart, and now she felt like maybe she would be able to do that before He returned.

This last year had been such a long journey, and she had learned so much about being still, leaning on His strength, not complaining, second chances, and staying hungry for the Word of God. The flesh, along with its emotions of hatred, anger, angst, and aggravation, had reared its ugly head way too many times. She would battle those minions and others sent her way for the rest of her life. The key was to fight, not to give in to those things that would rob her of her time in the Word of God and her walk with Him.

Just like the emissary of Stone's Corner said, "Wise choices lead to a less complicated life. A less complicated life leads to low drama. Low drama leads to wise choices."

Reba Jean looked at one last quote from Emissary Terry King, who stated, "We are all constantly influencing the life of someone else whether we want to or even realize we are doing it. Is your influence preparing that someone to spend an eternity in Heaven, or will they spend it in Hell?".

Epilogue

Book three was finished and had gone through preliminary personal edits. This book, which had originally been thought to take a year to even begin, instead took almost two years to finish. As Reba Jean went through the edits, she found that in the last two years, the same battles had to be consistently fought. That forgiveness had to be a treasure she used daily. The prevailing issues were not resolved. However, Reba Jean had learned a lot in the last two years. She was very careful not to complain. However, she now needed to practice patience and forgiveness.

Excerpt from Library of Lambency
Book 4 of the Lady Jane Chronicles

The heavy, cloying weight of darkness was smothering Lady Constance. That familiar whisper of evil caused her to withdraw within herself even further. She had to escape, yet she could not seem to claw her way back to the light. The voices of her family and friends seemed muffled and only made her feel violent anger.

She had promised God that she would not take her own life, but what good was her life to Him anyway? The weight of the darkness and all the voices swirling in her head finally overwhelmed her self-control, and she lashed out with vitriolic hostility to her family.

The next day, she finally dragged herself to church; she did not want to be there. The only one that seemed to understand and that she could half tolerate was Reba Jean. Reba Jean didn't flinch, at least not outwardly, when she declared how evil she had been to her family. Lady Constance hated these battles with her mental health, but giving in was never the solution.

If Reba Jean even knew how deep and dark these episodes were, she wouldn't hang around her. Lady Constance burst into angry tears at the thought, but yet, there was Reba Jean pushing through her stubborn wall of self-protection, praying with her, hugging her, willing her back into the arms of the Lamb, Who was her Light.

www.ingramcontent.com/pod-product-compliance
Lightning Source LLC
Chambersburg PA
CBHW020952180626
46814CB00003B/1054